P9-DFR-383

The Normal Heart

by Larry Kramer

Foreword by Joseph Papp

A SAMUEL FRENCH ACTING EDITION

SAMUEL FRENCH

FOUNDED 1830

NEW YORK HOLLYWOOD LONDON TORONTO

SAMUELFRENCH.COM

Copyright © 1985, 2011 by Larry Kramer
Foreword Copyright © 1985 by New American Library
Portion of "September 1, 1939" Copyright © 1940 by W.H. Auden
Reprinted from *The English Auden*, edited by Edward Mendelson by
permission of Random House, Inc.

ALL RIGHTS RESERVED

Cover Artwork by Paul Davis

CAUTION: Professionals and amateurs are hereby warned that *THE NORMAL HEART* is subject to a licensing fee. It is fully protected under the copyright laws of the United States of America, the British Commonwealth, including Canada, and all other countries of the Copyright Union. All rights, including professional, amateur, motion picture, recitation, lecturing, public reading, radio broadcasting, television and the rights of translation into foreign languages are strictly reserved. In its present form the play is dedicated to the reading public only.

The amateur and professional live stage performance rights to *THE NORMAL HEART* are controlled exclusively by Samuel French, Inc., and licensing arrangements and performance licenses must be secured well in advance of presentation. PLEASE NOTE that amateur licensing fees are set upon application in accordance with your producing circumstances. When applying for a licensing quotation and a performance license please give us the number of performances intended, dates of production, your seating capacity and admission fee. Licensing fees are payable one week before the opening performance of the play to Samuel French, Inc., at 45 W. 25th Street, New York, NY 10010.

Licensing fee of the required amount must be paid whether the play is presented for charity or gain and whether or not admission is charged.

Professional/Stock licensing fees quoted upon application to Samuel French, Inc.

For all other rights than those stipulated above, apply to: Casarotto Ramsay, Ltd., Waverley House, 7-12 Noel St., London W1F 86Q England; Attn: Tom Erhardt.

Particular emphasis is laid on the question of amateur or professional readings, permission and terms for which must be secured in writing from Samuel French, Inc.

Copying from this book in whole or in part is strictly forbidden by law, and the right of performance is not transferable.

Whenever the play is produced the following notice must appear on all programs, printing and advertising for the play: "Produced by special arrangement with Samuel French, Inc."

Due authorship credit must be given on all programs, printing and advertising for the play.

ISBN 978-0-573-61993-9   Printed in U.S.A.   #788

No one shall commit or authorize any act or omission by which the copyright of, or the right to copyright, this play may be impaired.

No one shall make any changes in this play for the purpose of production.

Publication of this play does not imply availability for performance. Both amateurs and professionals considering a production are strongly advised in their own interests to apply to Samuel French, Inc., for written permission before starting rehearsals, advertising, or booking a theatre.

No part of this book may be reproduced, stored in a retrieval system, or transmitted in any form, by any means, now known or yet to be invented, including mechanical, electronic, photocopying, recording, videotaping, or otherwise, without the prior written permission of the publisher.

MUSIC USE NOTE

Licensees are solely responsible for obtaining formal written permission from copyright owners to use copyrighted music in the performance of this play and are strongly cautioned to do so. If no such permission is obtained by the licensee, then the licensee must use only original music that the licensee owns and controls. Licensees are solely responsible and liable for all music clearances and shall indemnify the copyright owners of the play and their licensing agent, Samuel French, Inc., against any costs, expenses, losses and liabilities arising from the use of music by licensees.

IMPORTANT BILLING AND CREDIT REQUIREMENTS

All producers of *THE NORMAL HEART must* give credit to the Author of the Play in all programs distributed in connection with performances of the Play, and in all instances in which the title of the Play appears for the purposes of advertising, publicizing or otherwise exploiting the Play and/ or a production. The name of the Author *must* appear on a separate line on which no other name appears, immediately following the title and *must* appear in size of type not less than fifty percent of the size of the title type.

In addition the following credit *must* be given in all programs and publicity information distributed in association with this piece:

Original New York Production by
New York Shakespeare Festival
Produced by Joseph Papp

IMPORTANT CREDIT ACKNOWLEDGEMENT

It is the author's express wish that the following excerpt from W. H. Auden's poem be included in all programs along with the copyright acknowledgment of the poem *(see copyright page)*:

> The windiest militant trash
> Important Persons shout
> Is not so crude as our wish:
> What mad Nijinsky wrote
> About Diaghilev
> Is true of the normal heart;
> For the error bred in the bone
> Of each woman and each man
> Craves what it cannot have,
> Not universal love
> But to be loved alone.
>
> All I have is a voice
> To undo the folded lie,
> The romantic lie in the brain
> Of the sensual man-in-the-street
> And the lie of Authority
> Whose buildings grope the sky:
> There is no such thing as the State
> And no one exists alone;
> Hunger allows no choice
> To the citizen or the police;
> We must love one another or die.

— W.H. Auden
From "September 1, 1939"

THE NORMAL HEART opened on April 21, 1985 at the Public Theater in New York City, New York; a New York Shakespeare Festival Production, it was produced by Joseph Papp. The performance was directed by Michael Lindsay-Hogg, with sets by Eugene Lee and Keith Raywood, costumes by Bill Walker, lighting by Natasha Katz. The cast was as follows:

CRAIG DONNER	Michal Santoro
MICKEY MARCUS	Robert Dorfman
NED WEEKS	Brad Davis*
DAVID	Lawrence Lott
DR. EMMA BROOKNER	Concetta Tomei
BRUCE NILES	David Allen Brooks
FELIX TURNER	D. W. Moffett
BEN WEEKS	Phillip Richard Allen
TOMMY BOATWRIGHT	William DeAcutis
HIRAM KEEBLER	Lawrence Lott
GRADY	Michael Santoro
EXAMINING DOCTOR	Lawrence Lott
ORDERLY	Lawrence Lott
ORDERLY	Michael Santoro

* On August 19, 1985, Joel Grey assumed the role of Ned Weeks.

The revival of *THE NORMAL HEART* opened on Broadway in April 27, 2011 at the John Golden Theatre in New York City, New York; it was produced by Daryl Roth, Paul Boskind and Martian Entertainment; in association with Gregory Rae and Jayne Baron Sherman/Alexander Fraser. The performance was directed by Joel Grey and George C. Wolfe with set design by David Rockwell, lighting design by David Weiner, original music and sound design by David Van Tiegham, costume design by Martin Pakledinaz, and projection design by Batwin & Robin Productions, Inc. The production stage manager was Karen Armstrong. The cast was as follows:

CRAIG DONNER/GRADY	Luke MacFarlane
MICKEY MARCUS	Patrick Breen
NED WEEKS	Joe Mantello
DAVID	Wayne Alan Wilcox
DR. EMMA BROOKNER	Ellen Barkin
BRUCE NILES	Lee Pace
FELIX TURNER	John Benjamin Hickey
BEN WEEKS	Mark Harelik
TOMMY BOATWRIGHT	Jim Parsons
HIRAM KEEBLER/EXAMINING DOCTOR	Richard Topol

Understudies: Jordan Baker (**DR. EMMA BROOKNER**), Jon Levenson (**BEN WEEKS, EXAMINING DOCTOR, HIRAM KEEBLER, MICKEY MARCUS, NED WEEKS**), Lee Aaron Rosen (**BRUCE NILES, CRAIG DONNER, DAVID, GRADY, TOMMY BOATWRIGHT**).

CHARACTERS

CRAIG DONNER

MICKEY MARCUS

NED WEEKS

DAVID

DR. EMMA BROOKNER

BRUCE NILES

FELIX TURNER

BEN WEEKS

TOMMY BOATWRIGHT

HIRAM KEEBLER

GRADY

EXAMINING DOCTOR

ORDERLY

ORDERLY

TIME

The action of this play takes place between July 1981 and May 1984 in New York City.

SET

For the original 1985 production:

The New York Shakespeare Festival production at the Public Theater was conceived as exceptionally simple. Little furniture was used: a few wooden office chairs, a desk, a table, a sofa, and an old battered hospital gurney that found service as an examining table, a bench in City Hall, and a place for coats in the organization's old office. As the furniture found itself doing double-duty in different scenes, so did the doorways built into the set's back wall. In many instances, the actors used the theater itself for entrances and exits.

The walls of the set, made of construction-site plywood, were white-washed. Everywhere possible, on this set and upon the theater walls too, facts and figures and names were painted, in black, simple lettering.

Here are some of the things we painted on our walls:

1. Principal place was given to the latest total number of AIDS cases nationally: _____ AND COUNTING. (For example, on August 1,1985, the figure read 12,062.) As the Centers for Disease Control revise all figures regularly, so did we, crossing out old numbers and placing the new figure just beneath it.

2. EPIDEMIC OFFICIALLY DECLARED JUNE 5, 1981.

3. The total number of articles on the epidemic written by the following newspapers during the first ten months of 1984:

The San Francisco Chronicle. 163
The New York Times. 41
The Los Angeles Times 37
The Washington Post 24

4. During the first nineteen months of the epidemic, *The New York Times* wrote about it a total of seven times:

1. July 3, 1981, page 20 (41 cases reported by CDC)
2. August 29, 1981, page 9 (107 cases)
3. May 11, 1982, Section III, page 1 (335 cases)
4. June 18, 1982, Section II, page 8 (approximately 430 cases)
5. August 8, 1982, page 31 (505 cases)
6. January 6, 1983, Section II, page 17 (approximately 891 cases)
7. February 6, 1983, Magazine (The "Craig Claiborne" article.) (958 cases)

5. During the three months of the Tylenol scare in 1982, *The New York Times* wrote about it a total of 54 times:

October 1, 2, 3,4,5,6,7,8,9, 10, 11 , 12, 13, 14, 15, 16, 17, 18, 19,20,21,22,23,24,25,26, 27, 28, 29, 30, 31
November 2, 5, 6, 9, 12, 17,21,22,25
December 1, 2, 3, 4, 8, 10, 14, IS, 19, 25, 27, 28, 29, 30
Four of these articles appeared on the front page.
Total number of cases: 7.

6. Government research at the National Institutes of Health did not commence in reality until January, 1983, eighteen months after the same government had declared the epidemic.

7. Announcement of the discovery of "the virus" in France: January, 1983.
 Announcement of the "discovery" of "the virus" in Washington: April, 1984.

8. The public education budget for 1985 at the U.S. Department of Health and Human Services: $120,000.

9. Vast expanses of wall were covered with lists of names, much like the names one might find on a war memorial, such as the Vietnam Memorial in Washington.

For the 2011 Broadway revival:

Once again, minimal everything. The walls of the set were stark white with hardly visible facts and newspaper headlines. Slides were used to convey various location exteriors, NYU Medical Center, Ben's office building, Ned's booklined apartment. As the play proceeded, actors when not in a scene sat along the walls of the set in the shadows, watching the play. Felix and Ned are married, with Felix standing beside him, relieving us of a gurney, and he steps back into the shadows when he dies. At various times in the action lists of names of actual people are projected on the walls, the list short at first, and gradually growing in length until by the final moment the stage and all adjoining walls are covered with names.

SCENES AND APPROXIMATE DATES

ACT ONE

ACT TWO

ACKNOWLEDGMENTS

For the original 1985 production:

I am grateful to the following works of scholarship: "American Jewry During the Holocaust," a report edited by Seymour Maxwell Finger for the American Jewish Commission on the Holocaust, Hon. Arthur J. Goldberg, Chairman, March 1984, (the excerpt quoted herein is used by permission), *Israel in the Mind of America* by Peter Grose, Alfred A. Knopf, 1983; *American Jewry's Public Response to the Holocaust, /938-44*: An Examination Based upon Accounts in the Jewish Press and Periodical Literature, A Doctoral Dissertation by Haskel Lookstein, Yeshiva University, January 1979, University Microfilms, Ann Arbor, Michigan; *While Six Million Died, A Chronicle of American Apathy*, by Arthur D. Morse, copyright C 1967, The Overlook Press, Woodstock, New York, 1983; *The Abandonment of the Jews, America and the Holocaust 1941-1945*, by David S. Wyman, Pantheon Books, 1984.

I give special thanks and tribute to the late Dr. Linda J. Laubenstein.

I am exceptionally indebted to Gail Merrifield, the Director of Plays at the New York Shakespeare Festival, as I am to this remarkable organization's Literary Manager, Bill Hart, and to Michael Lindsay-Hogg for bravely birthing us.

There are no words splendid enough to contain and convey what Joseph Papp has meant to me, and to this play.

For the 2011 Broadway revival:

Daryl Roth, you are the greatest, most generous and loving producer any writer could ever have. There is no one to touch you. And everyone you have chosen to be around you – most particularly the indefatigable, loving Wendy Orshan, is as perfect as you are. You determined to find an audience for this play, and you did. You were especially determined to find a way to bring young people to see this play, and you did.

George Wolfe lives where only the greatest artists live, in some place far away and special, and private, and with luck, is sometimes dispatched preciously to mortal writers like me. George, I am so in awe of what you have done with my play and I want to work with you forever.

Together you have brought this great and perfect cast together, Joe and Hickey and Ellen and Lee and Jim and Patrick and Mark and Richard and Luke and Wayne.

Thank you all for the great gift of your talents.

Thank you too, Joel Grey, for starting this ball rolling. We might not have been here this time but for you.

What has been especially moving to me is that you have enabled so many of my people to come to learn our history. We have been a people singularly denied the right to know our history, and it continues to be my mission to bring this history to my people and the world.

So thank you all for helping me to do this in such a magnificent way.

—Larry Kramer

FOREWORD

Larry Kramer's *The Normal Heart* is a play in the great tradition of Western drama. In taking a burning social issue and holding it up to public and private scrutiny so that it reverberates with the social and personal implications of that issue, *The Normal Heart* reveals its origins in the theater of Sophocles, Euripides, and Shakespeare. In his moralistic fervor, Larry Kramer is a first cousin to nineteenth-century Ibsen and twentieth-century Odets and other radical writers of the 1930s. Yet, at the heart of *The Normal Heart*, the element that gives this powerful political play its essence, is love—love holding firm under fire, put to the ultimate test, facing and overcoming our greatest fear: death.

I love the ardor of this play, its howling, its terror and its kindness. It makes me very proud to have been its producer and caretaker.

—Joseph Papp, *1985*

For Norman J. Levy, who succeeded where all others failed.

To gay people everywhere, whom I love so.
The Normal Heart is our history.
It could not have been written had not so many of us so
needlessly died.
Learn from it and carry on the fight.
Let them know that we are a very special people,
an exceptional people.
And that our day will come.

Craig - sick

Mickey - friend

Emma - doctor

Ned - journalist

Felix - journalist for Gay community

Bruce - handsome

ACT ONE

Scene One

(The office of **DR. EMMA BROOKNER**. *Three men are in the waiting area:* **CRAIG DONNER, MICKEY MARCUS,** *and* **NED WEEKS**.*)*

CRAIG. *(after a long moment of silence)* I know something's wrong.

MICKEY. There's nothing wrong. When you're finished we'll go buy you something nice. What would you like?

CRAIG. We'll go somewhere nice to eat, okay? Did you see that guy in there's spots?

MICKEY. You don't have those. Do you?

CRAIG. No.

MICKEY. Then you don't have anything to worry about.

CRAIG. She said they can be inside you, too.

MICKEY. They're not inside you.

CRAIG. They're inside me.

MICKEY. Will you stop! Why are you convinced you're sick?

CRAIG. Where's Bruce? He's supposed to be here. I'm so lucky to have such a wonderful lover. I love Bruce so much, Mickey. I know something's wrong.

MICKEY. Craig, all you've come for is some test results. Now stop being such a hypochondriac.

CRAIG. I'm tired all the time. I wake up in swimming pools of sweat. Last time she felt me and said I was swollen. I'm all swollen, like something ready to explode. Thank you for coming with me, you're a good friend. Excuse me for being such a mess, Ned. I get freaked out when I don't feel well.

13

MICKEY. Everybody does.

*(**DAVID** comes out of **EMMA**'s office. There are highly visible purple lesions on his face. He wears a long-sleeved shirt. He goes to get his jacket, which he's left on one of the chairs.)*

DAVID. Whoever's next can go in.

CRAIG. Wish me luck.

MICKEY. *(hugging **CRAIG**)* Good luck.

*(**CRAIG** hugs him, then **NED**, and goes into **EMMA**'s office.)*

DAVID. They keep getting bigger and bigger and they don't go away. *(to **NED**)* I sold you a ceramic pig once at Maison France on Bleecker Street. My name is David.

NED. Yes, I remember. Somebody I was friends with then collects pigs and you had the biggest pig I'd ever seen outside of a real pig.

DAVID. I'm her twenty-eighth case and sixteen of them are dead. *(He leaves.)*

NED. Mickey, what the fuck is going on?

MICKEY. I don't know. Are you here to write about this?

NED. I don't know. What's wrong with that?

MICKEY. Nothing, I guess.

NED. What about you? What are you going to say? You're the one with the health column.

MICKEY. Well, I'll certainly write about it in the Native, but I'm afraid to put it in the stuff I write at work.

NED. What are you afraid of?

MICKEY. The city doesn't exactly show a burning interest in gay health. But at least I've still got my job: the Health Department has had a lot of cutbacks.

NED. How's John?

MICKEY. John? John who?

NED. You've had so many I never remember their last names.

MICKEY. Oh, you mean John. I'm with Gregory now. Gregory O'Connor.

NED. The old gay activist?

MICKEY. Old? He's younger than you are. I've been with Gregory for ten months now.

NED. Mickey, that's very nice.

MICKEY. He's not even Jewish. But don't tell my rabbi.

CRAIG. *(coming out of* **EMMA***'s office)* I'm going to die. That's the bottom line of what she's telling me. I'm so scared. I have to go home and get my things and come right back and check in. Mickey, please come with me. I hate hospitals. I'm going to die. Where's Bruce? I want Bruce.

*(**MICKEY** and **CRAIG** leave. **DR. EMMA BROOKNER** comes in from her office. She is in a motorized wheelchair. She is in her mid-to-late thirties.)*

EMMA. Who are you?

NED. I'm Ned Weeks. I spoke with you on the phone after the Times article.

EMMA. You're the writer fellow who's scared. I'm scared, too. I hear you've got a big mouth.

NED. Is big mouth a symptom?

EMMA. No, a cure. Come on in and take your clothes off.

NED. I only came to ask some questions.

EMMA. You're gay, aren't you? Take your clothes off.

*(Lights up on an examining table, center stage. **NED** starts to undress.)*

NED. Dr. Brookner, what's happening?

EMMA. I don't know.

NED. In just a couple of minutes you told two people I know something. The article said there isn't any cure.

EMMA. Not even any good clues yet. All I know is this disease is the most insidious killer I've ever seen or studied or heard about. And I think we're seeing only the tip of the iceberg. And I'm afraid it's on the rampage. I'm frightened nobody important is going to give a damn because it seems to be happening mostly to gay men. Who cares if a faggot dies? Does it occur to you to do anything about it. Personally?

NED. Me?

EMMA. Somebody's got to do something.

NED. Wouldn't it be better coming from you?

EMMA. Doctors are extremely conservative; they try to stay out of anything that smells political, and this smells. Bad. As soon as you start screaming you get treated like a nut case. Maybe you know that. And then you're ostracized and rendered worthless, just when you need cooperation most. Take off your socks.

(**NED**, *in his undershorts, is now sitting on the examining table.* **EMMA** *will now examine him, his skin particularly, starting with the bottom of his feet, feeling his lymph glands, looking at his scalp, into his mouth…*)

NED. Nobody listens for very long anyway. There's a new disease of the month every day.

EMMA. This hospital sent its report of our first cases to the medical journals over a year ago. *The New England Journal of Medicine* has finally published it, and last week, which brought you running, *The Times* ran something on some inside page. Very inside: page twenty. If you remember, Legionnaires' Disease, toxic shock, they both hit the front page of *The Times* the minute they happened. And stayed there until somebody did something. The front page of *The Times* has a way of inspiring action. Lie down.

NED. They won't even use the word "gay" unless it's in a direct quote. To them we're still homosexuals. That's like still calling blacks Negroes. *The Times* has always had trouble writing about anything gay.

EMMA. Then how is anyone going to know what's happening? And what precautions to take? Someone's going to have to tell the gay population fast.

NED. You've been living with this for over a year? Where's the Mayor? Where's the Health Department?

EMMA. They know about it. You have a Commissioner of Health who got burned with the Swine Flu epidemic, declaring an emergency when there wasn't one. The government appropriated $150 million for that mistake. You have a Mayor who's a bachelor and I assume afraid of being perceived as too friendly to anyone gay. And who is also out to protect a billion-dollar-a-year tourist industry. He's not about to tell the world there's an epidemic menacing his city. And don't ask me about the President. Is the Mayor gay?

NED. If he is, like J. Edgar Hoover, who would want him?

EMMA. Have you had any of the symptoms?

NED. I've had most of the sexually transmitted diseases the article said come first. A lot of us have. You don't know what it's been like since the sexual revolution hit this country. It's been crazy, gay or straight.

EMMA. What makes you think I don't know? Any fever, weight loss, night sweats, diarrhea, swollen glands, white patches in your mouth, loss of energy, shortness of breath, chronic cough?

NED. No. But those could happen with a lot of things, couldn't they?

EMMA. And purple lesions. Sometimes. Which is what I'm looking for. It's a cancer. There seems to be a strange reaction in the immune system. It's collapsed. Won't work. Won't fight. Which is what it's supposed to do. So most of the diseases my guys are coming down with – and there are some very strange ones – are caused by germs that wouldn't hurt a baby, not a baby in New York City anyway. Unfortunately, the immune system is the system we know least about. So where is this big mouth I hear you've got?

NED. I have more of a bad temper than a big mouth.

EMMA. Nothing wrong with that. Plenty to get angry about. Health is a political issue. Everyone's entitled to good medical care. If you're not getting it, you've got to fight for it. Open your mouth. Turn over. One of my staff told me you were well-known in the gay world and not afraid to say what you think. Is that true? I can't find any gay leaders. I tried calling several gay organizations. No one ever calls me back. Is anyone out there?

NED. There aren't any organizations strong enough to be useful, no. Dr. Brookner, nobody with a brain gets involved in gay politics. It's filled with the great unwashed radicals of any counterculture. That's why there aren't any leaders the majority will follow. Anyway, you're talking to the wrong person. What I think is politically incorrect.

EMMA. Why?

NED. Gay is good to that crowd, no matter what. There's no room for criticism, looking at ourselves critically.

EMMA. What's your main criticism?

NED. I hate how we play victim, when many of us, most of us, don't have to.

EMMA. Then you're exactly what's needed now.

NED. Nobody ever listens. We're not exactly a bunch that knows how to play follow the leader.

EMMA. Maybe they're just waiting for somebody to lead them.

NED. We are. What group isn't?

EMMA. You can get dressed. I can't find what I'm looking for.

NED. *(jumping down and starting to dress)* Needed? Needed for what? What is it exactly you're trying to get me to do?

EMMA. Tell gay men to stop having sex.

NED. What?

EMMA. Someone has to. Why not you?

NED. It is a preposterous request.

EMMA. It only sounds harsh. Wait a few more years, it won't sound so harsh.

NED. Do you realize that you are talking about millions of men who have singled out promiscuity to be their principal political agenda, the one they'd die before abandoning. How do you deal with that?

EMMA. Tell them they may die.

NED. You tell them!

EMMA. Are you saying you guys can't relate to each other in a nonsexual way?

NED. It's more complicated than that. For a lot of guys it's not easy to meet each other in any other way. It's a way of connecting – which becomes an addiction. And then they're caught in the web of peer pressure to perform and perform. Are you sure this is spread by having sex?

EMMA. Long before we isolated the hepatitis viruses we knew about the diseases they caused and had a good idea of how they got around. I think I'm right about this. I am seeing more cases each week than the week before. I figure that by the end of the year the number will be doubling every six months. That's something over a thousand cases by next June. Half of them will be dead. Your two friends I've just diagnosed? One of them will be dead. Maybe both of them.

NED. And you want me to tell every gay man in New York to stop having sex?

EMMA. Who said anything about just New York?

NED. You want me to tell every gay man across the country –

EMMA. Across the world! That's the only way this disease will stop spreading.

NED. Dr. Brookner, isn't that just a tiny bit unrealistic?

EMMA. Mr. Weeks, if having sex can kill you, doesn't anybody with half a brain stop fucking? But perhaps you've never lost anything. Good-bye.

(BRUCE NILES, *an exceptionally handsome man in his late thirties, rushes in carrying* CRAIG, *helped by* MICKEY.)

BRUCE. (*calling from off*) Where do I go? Where do I go?

EMMA. Quickly – put him on the table. What happened?

BRUCE. He was coming out of the building and he started running to me and then he…then he collapsed to the ground.

EMMA. What is going on inside your bodies!

(CRAIG starts to convulse. BRUCE, MICKEY, and NED restrain him.)

Gently.

(She takes a tongue depressor and holds CRAIG's tongue flat; she checks the pulse in his neck; she looks into his eyes for vital signs that he is coming around; CRAIG's convulsions stop.)

You the lover?

BRUCE. Yes.

EMMA. What's your name?

BRUCE. Bruce Niles, ma'am.

EMMA. How's your health?

BRUCE. Fine. Why – is it contagious?

EMMA. I think so.

MICKEY. Then why haven't you come down with it?

EMMA. *(moving toward a telephone)* Because it seems to have a very long incubation period and require close intimacy. Niles? You were Reinhard Holz's lover?

BRUCE. How did you know that? I haven't seen him in a couple of years.

EMMA. *(dialing the hospital emergency number)* He died three weeks ago. Brookner. Emergency. Set up a room immediately. *(hangs up)*

BRUCE. We were only boyfriends for a couple months.

MICKEY. It's like some sort of plague.

EMMA. There's always a plague. Of one kind or another. Mr. Weeks, I don't think your friend is going to live for very long.

Scene Two

(**FELIX TURNER'S** *desk at* The New York Times. **FELIX** *is always conservatively dressed, and is outgoing and completely masculine.*)

NED. *(entering, a bit uncomfortable and nervous)* Mr. Turner?

FELIX. Bad timing. *(looking up)* "Mister?"

NED. My name is Ned Weeks.

FELIX. You caught me at a rough moment. I have a deadline.

NED. I've been told you're gay and might be able to help get vital information in *The Times* about –

FELIX. You've been told? Who told you?

NED. The grapevine.

FELIX. Here I thought everyone saw me as the Burt Reynolds of West Forty-third Street. Please don't stop by and say hello to Mr. Sulzberger or Abe Rosenthal. What kind of vital information?

NED. You read the article about this new disease?

FELIX. Yes, I read it. I wondered how long before I'd hear from somebody. Why does everyone gay always think I run *The New York Times*? I can't help you...with this.

NED. I'm sorry to hear that. What would you suggest I do?

FELIX. Take your pick. I've got twenty-three parties, fourteen gallery openings, thirty-seven new restaurants, twelve new discos, one hundred and five spring collections... Anything sound interesting?

NED. No one here wants to write another article. I've talked to half a dozen reporters and editors and the guy who wrote the first piece.

FELIX. That's true. They won't want to write about it. And I can't. We're very departmentalized. You wouldn't want science to write about sweaters, would you?

NED. It is a very peculiar feeling having to go out and seek support from the straight world for something gay.

FELIX. I wouldn't know about that. I just write about gay designers and gay discos and gay chefs and gay rock stars and gay photographers and gay models and gay celebrities and gay everything. I just don't call them gay. Isn't that enough for doing my bit?

NED. No – I don't think it's going to be.

FELIX. I really do have a deadline and you wouldn't like me to get fired; who would write about us at all?

NED. Guys like you give me a pain in the ass. *(He starts out.)*

FELIX. You in the phone book?

NED. Yes.

Scene Three

(The law office of **BEN WEEKS, NED***'s older brother.* **BEN** *always dresses in a suit and tie, which* **NED** *never does. The brothers love each other a great deal;* **BEN***'s approval is essential to* **NED***.* **BEN** *is busy with some papers as* **NED** *waits for him.)*

BEN. Isn't it a bit early to get so worked up?

NED. Don't you be like that, too?

BEN. What have I done now?

NED. My friend Bruce and I went out to Fire Island and over the whole Labor Day weekend we collected the grand sum of $124.

BEN. You can read that as either an indication that it's a beginning and will improve, or as a portent that heads will stay in the sand. My advice is heads are going to stay in the sand.

NED. Because so many gay people are still in the closet?

BEN. Because people don't like to be frightened. When they get scared they don't behave well. It's called denial. *(giving* **NED** *some papers to sign)*

NED. *(signs them automatically)* What are these for?

BEN. Your account needs some more money. You never seem to do anything twice. One movie, one novel, one play…You know you are now living on your capital. I miss your being in the movie business. I like movies. *(unrolls some blueprints)*

NED. What are those?

BEN. I've decided to build a house.

NED. But the one you're in is terrific.

BEN. I just want to build me a dream house, so now I'm going to.

NED. It looks like a fortress. Does it have a moat? How much is it going to cost?

BEN. I suspect it'll wind up over a million bucks. But you're not to tell that to anyone. Not even Sarah. I've found some land in Greenwich, by a little river, completely protected by trees. Ned, it's going to be beautiful.

NED. Doesn't spending a million dollars on a house frighten you? It would scare the shit out of me. Even if I had it.

BEN. You can have a house anytime you want one. You haven't done badly.

NED. Do I detect a tinge of approval – from the big brother who always called me lemon?

BEN. Well, you were a lemon.

NED. I don't want a house.

BEN. Then why have you been searching for one in the country for so many years?

NED. It's no fun living in one alone.

BEN. There's certainly no law requiring you to do that. Is this…Bruce someone you're seeing?

NED. Why thank you for asking. Don't I wish. I see him. He just doesn't see me. Everyone's afraid of me anyway. I frighten them away. It's called the lemon complex.

BEN. I think you're the one who's scared.

NED. You've never said that before.

BEN. Yes, I have. You just didn't hear me. What's the worst thing that could happen to you.

NED. I'd spend a million bucks on a house. Look, Ben – please! *(He takes the blueprints from him.)* I've – we've started an organization to raise money and spread information and fight any way we can.

BEN. Fight who and what?

NED. I told you. There's this strange new disease…

BEN. You're not going to do that full-time?

NED. I just want to help it get started and I'll worry about how much time later on.

BEN. It sounds to me like another excuse to keep from writing.

NED. I knew you would say that. I was wondering…could your law firm incorporate us and get us tax-exempt status and take us on for free, what's it called, *pro bono?*

BEN. *Pro bono* for what? What are you going to do?

NED. I just told you – raise money and fight.

BEN. You have to be more specific than that. You have to have a plan.

NED. How about if we say we're going to become a cross between the League of Women Voters and the United States Marines? Is that a good-enough plan?

BEN. Well, we have a committee that decides this sort of thing. I'll have to put it to the committee.

NED. Why can't you just say yes?

BEN. Because we have a committee.

NED. But you're the senior partner and I'm your brother.

BEN. I fail to see what bearing that has on the matter. You're asking me to ask my partners to give up income that would ordinarily come into their pocket.

NED. I thought every law firm did a certain amount of this sort of thing – charity, worthy causes.

BEN. It's not up to me, however, to select just what these worthy causes might be.

NED. Well, that's a pity. What did you start the firm for?

BEN. That's one of our rules. It's a democratic firm.

NED. I think I like elitism better. When will you know?

BEN. Know what?

NED. Whether or not your committee wants to help dying faggots?

BEN. I'll put it to them at the next meeting.

NED. When is that?

BEN. When it is!

NED. When is it? Because if you're not going to help, I have to find somebody else.

BEN. You're more than free to do that.

NED. I don't want to do that! I want my brother's fancy famous big-deal straight law firm to be the first major New York law firm to do *pro bono* work for a gay cause. That would give me a great deal of pride. I'm sorry you can't see that. I'm sorry I'm still putting you in a position where you're ashamed of me. I thought we'd worked all that out years ago.

BEN. I am not ashamed of you! I told you I'm simply not free to take this on without asking my partners' approval at the next meeting.

NED. Why don't I believe that. When is the next meeting?

BEN. Next Monday. Can you wait until next Monday?

NED. Who else is on the committee?

BEN. What difference does that make?

NED. I'll lobby them. You don't seem like a very sure vote. Is Nelson on the committee? Norman Ivey? Harvey?

BEN. Norman and Harvey are.

NED. Good.

BEN. Okay? Lemon, where do you want to have lunch today? It's your turn to pay.

NED. It is not. I paid last week.

BEN. That's simply not true.

NED. Last week was…French. You're right. Do you know you're the only person in the world I can't get mad at and stay mad at. I think my world would come to an end without you. And then who would Ben talk to? *(He embraces BEN.)*

BEN. *(embracing back, a bit)* That's true.

NED. You're getting better at it.

Ben - Ned's brother, head of law firm,

Scene Four

(NED's apartment. It is stark, modern, all black and white. FELIX comes walking in from another room with a beer, and NED follows, carrying one, too.)

FELIX. That's quite a library in there. You read all those books?

NED. Why does everybody ask that?

FELIX. You have a whole room of 'em, you must want to get asked.

NED. I never thought of it that way. Maybe I do. Thank you. But no, of course I haven't. They go out of print and then you can't find them, so I buy them right away.

FELIX. I think you're going to have to face the fact you won't be able to read them all before you die.

NED. I think you're right.

FELIX. You know, I really used to like high tech, but I'm tired of it now. I think I want chintz back again. Don't be insulted.

NED. I'm not. I want chintz back again, too.

FELIX. So here we are – two fellows who want chintz back again. Excuse me for saying so, but you are stiff as starch.

NED. It's been a long time since I've had a date. This is a date, isn't it? *(FELIX nods.)* And on the rare occasion, I was usually the asker.

FELIX. That's what's thrown you off your style: I called and asked.

NED. Some style. Before any second date I usually receive a phone call that starts with "Now I don't know what you had in mind, but can't we just be friends?"

FELIX. No. Are you glad I'm here?

NED. Oh, I'm pleased as punch you're here. You're very good-looking. What are you doing here?

FELIX. I'll let that tiny bit of self-pity pass for the moment.

NED. It's not self-pity, it's nervousness.

FELIX. It's definitely self-pity. Do you think you're bad-looking?

NED. Where are you from?

FELIX. I'm from Oklahoma. I left home at eighteen and put myself through college. My folks are dead. My dad worked at the refinery in West Tulsa and my mom was a waitress at a luncheonette in Walgreen's.

NED. Isn't it amazing how a kid can come out of all that and wind up on *The Times* dictating taste and style and fashion to the entire world?

FELIX. And we were talking so nicely.

NED. Talking is not my problem. Shutting up is my problem. And keeping my hands off you.

FELIX. You don't have to keep your hands off me. You have very nice hands. Do you have any awkward sexual tendencies you want to tell me about, too? That I'm not already familiar with?

NED. What are you familiar with?

FELIX. I have found myself pursuing men who hurt me. Before minor therapy. You're not one of those?

NED. No, I'm the runner. I was the runner. Until major therapy. After people who didn't want me and away from people who do.

FELIX. Isn't it amazing how a kid can come out of all that analyzing everything incessantly down to the most infinitesimal neurosis and still be all alone?

NED. I'm sorry you don't like my Dr. Freud. Another aging Jew who couldn't get laid.

FELIX. Just relax. You'll get laid.

NED. I try being laid-back, assertive, funny, butch…What's the point? I don't think there are many gay relationships that work out anyway.

FELIX. It's difficult to imagine you being laid-back. I know a lot of gay relationships that are working out very well.

NED. I guess I never see them.

FELIX. That's because you're a basket case.

NED. Fuck off.

FELIX. What's the matter? Don't you think you're attractive? Don't you like your body?

NED. I don't think anybody really likes their body. I read that somewhere.

FELIX. You know my fantasy has always been to go away and live by the ocean and write twenty-four novels, living with someone just like you with all these books who of course will be right there beside me writing your own twenty-four novels.

NED. *(after a beat)* Me, too.

FELIX. Harold Robbins marries James Michener.

NED. How about Tolstoy and Charles Dickens?

FELIX. As long as Kafka doesn't marry Dostoevsky.

NED. Dostoevsky is my favorite writer.

FELIX. I'll have to try him again.

NED. If you really feel that way, why do you write all that society and party and fancy-ball-gown bullshit?

FELIX. Here we go again. I'll bet you gobble it up every day.

NED. I do. I also know six people who've died. When I came to you a few weeks ago, it was only one.

FELIX. I'm sorry. Is that why you agreed to this date?

NED. Do you know that when Hitler's Final Solution to eliminate the Polish Jews was first mentioned in *The Times* it was on page twenty-eight. And on page six of *The Washington Post*. And *The Times* and *The Post* were owned by Jews. What causes silence like that? Why didn't the American Jews help the German Jews get out? Their very own people! Scholars are finally writing honestly about this – I've been doing some research – and it's damning to everyone who was here then: Jewish leadership for being totally ineffective; Jewish organizations for constantly fighting among themselves, unable to cooperate even in the face of death: Zionists versus non-Zionists, Rabbi Wise against Rabbi Silver...

FELIX. Is this some sort of special way you talk when you don't want to talk? We were doing so nicely.

NED. We were?

FELIX. Wasn't there an awful lot of anti-Semitism in those days? Weren't Jews afraid of rubbing people's noses in too much shit?

NED. Yes, everybody has a million excuses for not getting involved. But aren't there moral obligations, moral commandments to try everything possible? Where were the Christian churches, the Pope, Churchill? And don't get me started on Roosevelt...How I was brought up to worship him, all Jews were. A clear statement from him would have put everything on the front pages, would have put Hitler on notice. But his administration did its best to stifle publicity at the same time as they clamped down immigration laws forbidding entry, and this famous haven for the oppressed became as inaccessible as Tibet. The title of Treasury Secretary Morgenthau's report to Roosevelt was "Acquiescence of This Government in the Murder of the Jews," which he wrote in 1944. Dachau was opened in 1933. Where was everybody for eleven years? And then it was too late.

FELIX. This is turning out to be a very romantic evening.

NED. And don't tell me how much you can accomplish working from the inside. Jewish leaders, relying on their contacts with people in high places, were still, quietly, from the inside, attempting to persuade them when the war was over.

FELIX. What do you want me to say? Do you ever take a vacation?

NED. A vacation. I forgot. That's the great goal, isn't it. A constant Fire Island vacation. Party, party; fuck, fuck. Maybe you can give me a few trendy pointers on what to wear.

FELIX. Boy, you really have a bug up your ass. Look, I'm
not going to tell them I'm gay and could I write about
the few cases of a mysterious disease that seems to be
standing in the way of your kissing me even though
there must be half a million gay men in this city who
are fine and healthy. Let us please acknowledge the
law of averages. And this is not World War Two. The
numbers are nowhere remotely comparable. And all
analogies to the Holocaust are tired, overworked,
boring, probably insulting, possibly true, and a major
turnoff.

NED. Are they?

FELIX. Boy, I think I've found myself a real live weird one. I
had no idea. *(pause)* Hey, I just called you weird.

NED. You are not the first.

FELIX. You've never had a lover, have you?

NED. Where did you get that from?

FELIX. Have you? Wow.

NED. I suppose you've had quite a few.

FELIX. I had a very good one for a number of years, thank
you. He was older than I was and he found someone
younger.

NED. So you like them older. You looking for a father?

FELIX. No, I am not looking for a father! God, you are
relentless. And as cheery as Typhoid Mary.

(NED *comes over to* FELIX. *Then he leans over and kisses
him. The kiss becomes quite intense. Then* NED *breaks
away, jumps up, and begins to walk around nervously.*)

NED. The American Jews knew exactly what was happening, but everything was down played and stifled. Can
you imagine how effective it would have been if every
Jew in America had marched on Washington? Proudly!
Who says I want a lover? Huh!? I mean, why doesn't
anybody believe me when I say I do not want a lover?

FELIX. You are fucking crazy. Jews, Dachau, Final Solution – what kind of date is this! I don't believe anyone in the whole wide world doesn't want to be loved. Ned, you don't remember me, do you? We've been in bed together. We made love. We talked. We kissed. We cuddled. We made love again. I keep waiting for you to remember, something, anything. But you don't!

NED. How could I not remember you?

FELIX. I don't know.

NED. Maybe if I saw you naked.

FELIX. It's okay as long as we treat each other like whores. It was at the baths a few years ago. You were busy cruising some blond number and I stood outside your door waiting for you to come back and when you did you gave me such an inspection up and down you would have thought I was applying for the CIA.

NED. And then what?

FELIX. I just told you. We made love twice. I thought it was lovely. You told me your name was Ned, that when you were a child you read a Philip Barry play called *Holiday* where there was a Ned, and you immediately switched from...Alexander? I teased you for taking such a Wasp, up-in-Connecticut-for-the-weekend-name, and I asked what you did, and you answered something like you'd tried a number of things, and I asked you if that had included love, which is when you said you had to get up early in the morning. That's when I left. But I tossed you my favorite go-fuck-yourself yourself when you told me "I really am not in the market for a lover" – men do not just naturally not love – they learn not to. I am not a whore. I just sometimes make mistakes and look for love in the wrong places. And I think you're a bluffer. Your novel was all about a man desperate for love and a relationship, in a world filled with nothing but casual sex.

NED. Do you think we could start over?

FELIX. Maybe.

Scene Five

(NED's *apartment.* **MICKEY, BRUCE,** *and* **TOMMY BOATWRIGHT,** *a Southerner in his late twenties, are stuffing envelopes with various inserts and then packing them into cartons. Beer and pretzels.*)

MICKEY. *(calling off)* Ned, Gregory says hello and he can't believe you've turned into an activist. He says where were you fifteen years ago when we needed you.

NED. *(coming in with a tray with more beer)* You tell Gregory fifteen years ago no self-respecting faggot would have anything to do with you guys.

TOMMY. I was twelve years old.

BRUCE. We're not activists.

MICKEY. If you're not an activist, Bruce, then what are you?

BRUCE. Nothing. I'm only in this until it goes away.

MICKEY. You know, the battle against the police at Stonewall was won by transvestites. We all fought like hell. It's you Brooks Brothers guys who –

BRUCE. That's why I wasn't at Stonewall. I don't have anything in common with those guys, girls, whatever you call them. Ned, Robert Stokes has it. He called me today.

NED. At Glenn Fitzsimmons' party the other night, I saw one friend there I knew was sick, I learned about two others, and then walking home I bumped into Richie Faro, who told me he'd just been diagnosed.

MICKEY. Richie Faro?

NED. All this on Sixth Avenue between Nineteenth and Eighth Streets.

MICKEY. Richie Faro – gee, I haven't seen him since Stonewall. I think we even had a little affairlet.

BRUCE. Are you a transvestite?

MICKEY. No, but I'll fight for your right to be one.

BRUCE. I don't want to be one!

MICKEY. I'm worried this organization might only attract white bread and middle-class. We need blacks...

TOMMY. Right on!

MICKEY. ...and...how do you feel about Lesbians?

BRUCE. Not very much. I mean, they're...something else.

MICKEY. I wonder what they're going to think about all this? If past history is any guide, there's never been much support by either half of us for the other. Tommy, are you a Lesbian?

TOMMY. *(as he exits into the kitchen)* I have done and seen everything.

NED. *(to* **BRUCE***)* How are you doing?

BRUCE. I'm okay now. I forgot to thank you for sending flowers .

NED. That's okay.

BRUCE. Funny – my mother sent flowers. We've never even talked about my being gay. I told her Craig died. I guess she knew.

NED. I think mothers somehow always know. Would you like to have dinner next week, maybe see a movie?

BRUCE. *(uncomfortable when* **NED** *makes advances)* Actually... it's funny...it happened so fast. You know Albert? I've been seeing him.

NED. That guy in the Calvin Klein ads? Great!

*(***TOMMY** *returns with another carton of envelopes and boxes.)*

BRUCE. I don't think I like to be alone. I've always been with somebody.

MICKEY. *(looking up from his list-checking)* We have to choose a president tonight, don't forget. I'm not interested. And what about a board of directors?

BRUCE. *(looking at one of the flyers)* Mickey, how did you finally decide to say it? I didn't even look.

MICKEY. I just said the best medical knowledge, which admittedly isn't very much, seems to feel that a virus has landed in our community. It could have been any community, but it landed in ours. I guess we just got in the way. Boy, are we going to have paranoia problems.

NED. *(looking at a flyer)* That's all you said?

MICKEY. See what I mean? No, I also put in the benefit dance announcement and a coupon for donations.

NED. What about the recommendations?

MICKEY. I recommend everyone should donate a million dollars. How are we going to make people realize this is not just a gay problem? If it happens to us, it can happen to anybody.

NED. *(who has read the flyer and is angry)* Mickey, I thought we talked this out on the phone. We must tell everybody what Emma wants us to tell them.

MICKEY. She wants to tell them so badly she won't lend her name as recommending it. *(to the others)* This is what Ned wrote for me to send out. "If this doesn't scare the shit out of you, and rouse you to action, gay men may have no future here on earth." Neddie, I think that's a bit much.

BRUCE. You'll scare everybody to death!

NED. Shake up. What's wrong with that? This isn't something that can be force-fed gently; it won't work. Mickey neglected to read my first sentence.

MICKEY. "It's difficult to write this without sounding alarmist or scared." Okay, but then listen to this: "I am sick of guys moaning that giving up careless sex until this blows over is worse than death…I am sick of guys who can only think with their cocks…I am sick of closeted gays. It's 1982 now, guys, when are you going to come out? By 1984 you could be dead."

BRUCE. You're crazy.

NED. Am I? There are almost five hundred cases now. Okay, if we're not sending it out, I'll get *The Native* to run it.

BRUCE. But we can't tell people how to live their lives! We can't do that. And besides, the entire gay political platform is fucking. We'd get it from all sides.

NED. You make it sound like that's all that being gay means.

BRUCE. That's all it does mean!

MICKEY. It's the only thing that makes us different.

NED. I don't want to be considered different.

BRUCE. Neither do I, actually.

MICKEY. Well, I do.

BRUCE. Well, you are!

NED. Why is it we can only talk about our sexuality, and so relentlessly? You know, Mickey, all we've created is generations of guys who can't deal with each other as anything but erections. We can't even get a meeting with the mayor's gay assistant!

TOMMY. I'm very interested in setting up some sort of services for the patients. We've got to start thinking about them.

BRUCE. *(whispering to NED)* Who's he?

TOMMY. He heard about you and he found you and here he is. My name is Tommy Boatwright… *(to NED)* Why don't you write that down? Tommy Boatwright. In real life, I'm a hospital administrator. And I'm a Southern bitch.

NED. Welcome to gay politics.

BRUCE. Ned, I won't have anything to do with any organization that tells people how to live their lives.

NED. It's not telling them. It's a recommendation.

MICKEY. With a shotgun to their heads.

BRUCE. It's interfering with their civil rights.

MICKEY. Fucking as a civil right? Don't we just wish.

TOMMY. What if we put it in the form of a recommendation from gay doctors? So that way we're just the conduit.

NED. I can't get any gay doctor to go on record and say publicly what Emma wants.

BRUCE. *(suddenly noticing an envelope)* What the fuck is this?

MICKEY. Unh, oh!

BRUCE. Look at this! Was this your idea?

NED. I'm looking. I'm not seeing.

NED. What don't I see?

MICKEY. What we put for our return address.

NED. You mean the word gay is on the envelope?

BRUCE. You're damn right. Instead of just the initials. Who did it?

NED. Well, maybe it was Pierre who designed it. Maybe it was a mistake at the printers. But it is the name we chose for this organization...

BRUCE. You chose. I didn't want "gay" in it.

MICKEY. No, we all voted. That was one of those meetings when somebody actually showed up.

BRUCE. We can't send them out.

NED. We have to if we want anybody to come to the dance. They were late from the printers as it is.

BRUCE. We can go through and scratch out the word with a Magic Marker.

NED. Ten thousand times? Look, I feel sympathy for young guys still living at home on Long Island with their parents, but most men getting these...Look at you, in your case what difference does it make? You live alone, you own your own apartment, your mother lives in another state...

BRUCE. What about my mailman?

(**MICKEY** *lets out a little laughing yelp, then clears his throat.*)

NED. You don't expect me to take that seriously?

BRUCE. Yes, I do!

NED. What about your doorman?

BRUCE. What about him?

NED. Why don't you worry about him? All those cute little Calvin Klein numbers you parade under his nose, he thinks you're playing poker with the boys?

BRUCE. You don't have any respect for anyone who doesn't think like you do, do you?

NED. Bruce, I don't agree with you about this. I think it's imperative that we all grow up now and come out of the closet.

MICKEY. Ladies, behave! Ned, you don't think much of our sexual revolution. You say it all the time.

NED. No, I say I don't think much of promiscuity. And what's that got to do with gay envelopes?

MICKEY. But you've certainly done your share.

NED. That doesn't mean I approve of it or like myself for doing it.

MICKEY. But not all of us feel that way. And we don't like to hear the word "promiscuous" used pejoratively.

BRUCE. Or so publicly.

NED. Where the world can hear it, Bruce?

MICKEY. Sex is liberating. It's always guys like you who've never had one who are always screaming about relationships, and monogamy and fidelity and holy matrimony. What are you, a closet straight?

NED. Mickey, more sex isn't more liberating. And having so much sex makes finding love impossible.

MICKEY. Neddie, dahling, do not put your failure to find somebody on the morality of all the rest of us.

NED. Mickey, dahling, I'm just saying what I think! It's taken me twenty years of assorted forms of therapy in various major world capitals to be able to do so without guilt, fear, or giving a fuck if anybody likes it or not.

TOMMY. I'll buy that!

NED. Thank you.

BRUCE. But not everyone's so free to say what they think!

MICKEY. Or able to afford so much therapy. Although God knows I need it. *(looking at his watch)* Look, it's late, and we haven't elected our president. Ned, I think it should be...Bruce. Everybody knows him and likes him and...I mean, everybody expects you to –

NED. You mean he's popular and everybody's afraid of me.

MICKEY. Yes.

TOMMY. No.

MICKEY. No.

TOMMY. No, what it means is that you have a certain kind of energy that's definitely needed, but Bruce has a... presence that might bring people together in a way you can't.

NED. What's that mean?

TOMMY. It means he's gorgeous – and all the kids on Christopher Street and Fire Island will feel a bit more comfortable following him.

NED. Just like high school.

TOMMY & MICKEY. Yes!

NED. Follow him where?

TOMMY. *(putting his arm around him)* Well, honey, why don't we have a little dinner and I'll tell you all about it – and more.

NED. Uhn, thanks, I'm busy.

TOMMY. Forever? Well, that's too bad. I wanted to try my hand at smoothing out your rough edges.

MICKEY. Good luck.

NED. *(to BRUCE)* Well, it looks like you're the president.

BRUCE. I don't think I want this.

NED. Oh, come on, you're gorgeous – and we're all going to follow you.

BRUCE. Fuck you. I accept.

NED. Well, fuck you, congratulations.

TOMMY. There are going to be a lot of scared people out there needing someplace to call for information. I'd be interested in starting some sort of telephone hotline.

BRUCE. *(his first decision in office)* Unh…sure. Just prepare a detailed budget and let me see it before you make any commitments.

MICKEY. *(to* **NED***)* Don't you feel in safe hands already?

TOMMY. *(to* **BRUCE***)* What is it you do for a living, if I may ask?

BRUCE. I'm a vice-president of Citibank.

TOMMY. That's nothing to be shy about, sugar. You invented the Cash Machine. *(picking up an envelope)* So, are we mailing these out or what?

BRUCE. What do you think?

TOMMY. I'll bet nobody even notices.

BRUCE. Oh, there will be some who notice. Okay.

TOMMY. Okay? Okay! Our first adult compromise. Thank y'all for your cooperation.

*(***FELIX***, carrying a shopping bag, lets himself in with his own key.* **NED** *goes to greet him.)*

NED. Everybody, this is Felix. Bruce, Tommy, Mickey. Bruce just got elected president.

FELIX. My condolences. Don't let me interrupt. Anybody wants any Balducci gourmet ice cream – it's eighteen bucks a pint?

*(***NED** *proudly escorts* **FELIX** *into the kitchen.)*

MICKEY. It looks like Neddie's found a boyfriend.

BRUCE. Thank God, now maybe he'll leave me alone.

TOMMY. Shit, he's got his own key. It looks like I signed on too late.

BRUCE. I worry about Ned. I mean, I like him a lot, but his style is so…confrontational. We could get into a lot of trouble with him.

TOMMY. Honey, he looks like a pretty good catch to me. We could get into a lot of trouble without him.

(**NED** *comes back and starts clearing up.*)

MICKEY. I'm going home. My Gregory, he burns dinner every night, and when I'm late, he blames me.

BRUCE. *(to* **NED***)* My boss doesn't know and he hates gays. He keeps telling me fag jokes and I keep laughing at them.

NED. Citibank won't fire you for being gay. And if they did. we could make such a stink that every gay customer in New York would leave them. Come on, Bruce – you used to be a fucking Green Beret!

TOMMY. Goodness!

BRUCE. But I love my job. I supervise a couple thousand people all over the country and my investments are up to twenty million now.

MICKEY. I'm leaving. *(He hefts a carton and starts out.)*

BRUCE. Wait, I'm coming. *(to* **NED***)* I just think we have to stay out of anything political.

NED. And I think it's going to be impossible to pass along any information or recommendation that isn't going to be considered political by somebody.

TOMMY. And I think this is not an argument you two boys are going to settle tonight.

(**BRUCE** *picks up a big carton and heads out.*)

TOMMY. *(who has waited impatiently for* **BRUCE** *to leave so he can be alone with* **NED***)* I just wanted to tell you I really admire your writing…and your passion…

(*As* **FELIX** *reenters from the kitchen,* **TOMMY** *drops his flirtatious tone.*)

…and what you've been saying and doing, and it's because of you I'm here. *(to* **FELIX***)* Take care this good man doesn't burn out. Good night. *(He leaves.)*

NED. We just elected a president who's in the closet. I lost every argument. And I'm the only screamer among them. Oh, I forgot to tell them – I'm getting us something on the local news.

FELIX. Which channel?

NED. It's not TV, it's radio...It's a start.

FELIX. Ned, I think you should have been president.

NED. I didn't really want it. I've never been any good playing on a team. I like stirring things up my own. Bruce will be a good president. I'll shape him up. Where's the ice cream? Do you think I'm crazy?

FELIX. I certainly do. That's why I'm here.

NED. I'm so glad.

FELIX. That I'm here?

NED. That you think I'm crazy. *(They kiss.)*

Scene Six

(BEN's office. In a corner is a large model of the new house under a cloth cover.)

BEN. You got your free legal work from my firm; now I'm not going to be on your board of directors, too.

NED. I got our free legal work from your firm by going to Norman and he said, "Of course, no problem." I asked him, "Don't you have to put it before your committee?" And he said, "Nah, I'll just tell them we're going to do it."

BEN. Well…you got it.

NED. All I'm asking for is the use of your name. You don't have to do a thing. This is an honorary board. For the stationary.

BEN. Ned, come on – it's your cause, not mine.

NED. That is just an evasion!

BEN. It is not. I don't ask you to help me with the Larchmont school board, do I?

NED. But I would if you asked me.

BEN. But I don't.

NED. Would you be more interested if you thought this was a straight disease?

BEN. It has nothing to do with your being gay.

NED. Of course it has. What else has it got to do with?

BEN. I've got other things to do.

NED. But I'm telling you you don't have to do a thing!

BEN. The answer is No.

NED. It's impossible to get this epidemic taken seriously. I wrote a letter to the gay newspaper and some guy wrote in, "Oh there goes Ned Weeks again; he wants us all to die so he can say 'I told you so.'"

BEN. He sounds like a crazy.

NED. It kept me up all night.

BEN. Then you're crazy, too.

NED. I ran into an old friend I hadn't seen in years in the subway, and I said, "Hello, how are you?" He started screaming, "You're giving away all our secrets, you're painting us as sick, you're destroying homosexuality" and then he tried to slug me. Right there in the subway. Under Bloomingdale's.

BEN. Another crazy.

NED. We did raise $50,000 at our dance last week. That's more money than any gay organization has ever raised at one time in this city before.

BEN. That's wonderful, Ned. So you must be beginning to do something right.

NED. And I made a speech appealing for volunteers and we got over a hundred people to sign up, including a few women. And I've got us on Donahue. I'm going to be on Donahue with a doctor and a patient.

BEN. Don't tell your mother.

NED. Why not?

BEN. She's afraid someone is going to shoot you.

(**BEN** *rolls the model house stage center and pulls off the cover.*)

NED. What about you? Aren't you afraid your corporate clients will say, "Was that your faggot brother I saw on TV?" Excuse me – is this a bad time? You seem preoccupied.

BEN. Do I? I'm sorry. A morning with the architect is enough to shake me up a little bit. It's going to cost more than I thought.

NED. More?

BEN. Twice as much.

NED. Two million?

BEN. I can handle it.

NED. You can? That's very nice. You know, Ben, one of these days I'll make you agree that over twenty million men and women are not all here on this earth because of something requiring the services of a psychiatrist.

BEN. Oh, it's up to twenty million now, is it? Every time we have this discussion, you up the ante.

NED. We haven't had this discussion in years, Ben. And we grow, just like everybody else.

BEN. Look, I try to understand. I read stuff. *(picking up a copy of Newsweek, with "Gay America" on the cover)* I open magazines and I see pictures of you guys in leather and chains and whips and black masks, with captions saying this is a social worker, this is a computer analyst, this is a schoolteacher – and I say to myself, "This isn't Ned."

NED. No, it isn't. It isn't most of us. You know the media always dramatizes the most extreme. Do you think we all wear dresses, too?

BEN. Don't you?

NED. Me, personally? No, I do not.

BEN. But then you tell me how you go to the bathhouses and fuck blindly, and to me that's not so different from this. You guys don't seem to understand why there are rules, and regulations, guidelines, responsibilities. You guys have a dreadful image problem.

NED. I know that! That's what has to be changed. That's why it's so important to have people like you supporting us. You're a respected person. You already have your dignity.

BEN. We better decide where we're going to eat lunch and get out of here. I have an important meeting.

NED. Do you? How important? I've asked for your support.

BEN. In every area I consider important you have my support.

NED. In some place deep inside of you you still think I'm sick. Isn't that right? Okay. Define it for me. What do you mean by "sick"? Sick unhealthy? Sick perverted? Sick I'll get over it? Sick to be locked up?

BEN. I think you've adjusted to life quite well.

NED. All things considered? *(BEN nods.)* In the only area I consider important I don't have your support at all. The single-minded determination of all you people to forever see us as sick helps keep us sick.

BEN. I saw how unhappy you were!

NED. So were you! You wound up going to shrinks, too. We grew up side by side. We both felt pretty much the same about Mom and Pop. I refuse to accept for one more second that I was damaged by our childhood while you were not.

BEN. But we all don't react the same way to the same thing.

NED. That's right. So I became a writer and you became a lawyer. I'll agree to the fact that I have any number of awful character traits. But not to the fact that whatever they did to us as kids automatically made me sick and gay while you stayed straight and healthy.

BEN. Well, that's the difference of opinion we have over theory.

NED. But your theory turns me into a man from Mars. My theory doesn't do that to you.

BEN. Are you suggesting it was wrong of me to send you into therapy so young? I didn't think you'd stay in it forever.

NED. I didn't think I'd done anything wrong until you sent me into it. Ben, you know you mean more to me than anyone else in the world; you always have. Although I think I've finally found someone I like...Don't you understand?

BEN. No, I don't understand.

NED. You've got to say it. I'm the same as you. Just say it. Say it!

BEN. No, you're not. I can't say it.

NED. *(He is heartbroken.)* Every time I lose this fight it hurts more. I don't want to have lunch. I'll see you. *(He starts out.)*

BEN. Come on, lemon, I still love you. Sarah loves you. Our children. Our cat. Our dog...

NED. You think this is a joke!

BEN. *(angry)* You have my love and you have my legal advice and my financial supervision. I can't give you the courage to stand up and say to me that you don't give a good healthy fuck what I think. Please stop trying to wring some admission of guilt out of me. I am truly happy that you've met someone. It's about time. And I'm sorry your friends are dying...

NED. If you're so sorry, join our honorary board and say you're sorry out loud!

BEN. My agreeing you were born just like I was born is not going to help save your dying friends.

NED. Funny – that's exactly what I think will help save my dying friends.

BEN. Ned – you can be gay and you can be proud no matter what I think. Everybody is oppressed by somebody else in some form or another. Some of us learn how to fight back, with or without the help of others, despite their opinions, even those closest to us. And judging from this mess your friends are in, it's imperative that you stand up and fight to be prouder than ever.

NED. Can't you see that I'm trying to do that? Can't your perverse ego proclaiming its superiority see that I'm trying to be proud? You can only find room to call yourself normal.

BEN. You make me sound like I'm the enemy.

NED. I'm beginning to think that you and your straight world are our enemy. I am furious with you, and with myself and with every goddamned doctor who ever told me I'm sick and interfered with my loving a man. I'm trying to understand why nobody wants to hear we're dying, why nobody wants to help, why my own brother doesn't want to help. Two million dollars – for a house! We can't even get twenty-nine cents from the city. You still think I'm sick, and I simply cannot allow that any longer. I will not speak to you again until you accept me as your equal. Your healthy equal. Your brother! *(He runs out.)*

Scene Seven

*(NED's apartment. **FELIX**, working on an article, is spread out on the floor with books, note pad, comforter, and pillows. NED enters, eating from a pint of ice cream.)*

NED. At the rate I'm going, no one in this city will be talking to me in about three more weeks. I had another fight with Bruce today. I slammed the phone down on him. I don't know why I do that – I'm never finished saying what I want to, so I just have to call him back, during which I inevitably work myself up into another frenzy and hang up on him again. That poor man doesn't know what to do with me. I don't think people like me work at Citibank.

FELIX. Why can't you see what an ordinary guy Bruce is? I know you think he has hidden qualities, if you just give him plant food he'll grow into the fighter you are. He can't. All he's got is a lot of good looking Pendleton shirts.

NED. I know there are better ways to handle him. I just can't seem to. This epidemic is killing friendships, too. I can't even talk to my own brother. Why doesn't he call me?

FELIX. There's the phone.

NED. Why do I always have to do the running back?

FELIX. All you ever eat is desserts.

NED. Sugar is the most important thing in my life. All the rest is just to stay alive.

FELIX. What was the fight about?

NED. Which fight?

FELIX. Bruce.

NED. Pick a subject.

FELIX. How many do you know now?

NED. Forty…dead. That's too many for one person to know. Curt Morgan, this guy I went to Yale with, just died.

FELIX. Emerick Nolan – he gave me my first job on *The Washington Post.*

NED. Bruce is getting paranoid: now his lover, Albert, isn't feeling well. Bruce is afraid he's giving it to everyone.

FELIX. Maybe it isn't paranoia. Maybe what we do with our lovers is what we should be thinking about most of all. *(The phone rings.* **NED** *answers it.)*

NED. Hello. Hold on. *(locating some pages and reading from them into the phone)* "It is no secret that I consider the Mayor to be, along with *The Times,* the biggest enemy gay men and women must contend with in New York. Until the day I die I will never forgive this newspaper and this Mayor for ignoring this epidemic that is killing so many of my friends . If…" All right, here's the end. "And every gay man who refuses to come forward now and fight to save his own life is truly helping to kill the rest of us. How many of us have to die before you get scared off your ass and into action?" …Thank you. *(He hangs up.)* I hear it's becoming known as the Ned Weeks School of Outrage.

FELIX. Who was that?

NED. Felix, I'm orchestrating this really well. I know I am. We have over six hundred volunteers now. I've got us mentioned in *Time, Newsweek,* the evening news on all three networks, both local and national, English and French and Canadian and Australian TV, all the New York area papers except *The Times* and *The Voice…*

FELIX. You're doing great.

NED. But they don't support me! Bruce…this fucking board of directors we put together, all friends of mine – every single one of them yelled at me for two solid hours last night. They think I'm creating a panic, I'm using it to make myself into a celebrity – not one of them will appear on TV or be interviewed, so I do it all by default; so now I'm accused of being self-serving, as if it's fun getting slugged on the subway.

FELIX. They're beginning to get really frightened. You are becoming a leader. And you love to fight.

NED. What? I love it?

FELIX. Yes!

NED. I love to fight? Moi?

FELIX. Yes, you do, and you're having a wonderful time.

NED. Yes, I am. *(meaning* **FELIX***)*

FELIX. I did speak to one of our science reporters today.

NED. *(delighted)* Felix! What did he say?

FELIX. He's gay, too, and afraid they'll find out. Don't yell at me! Ned, I tried. All those shrinks, they must have done something right to you.

NED. *(giving* **FELIX** *a kiss with each name)* Dr. Malev, Dr. Ritvo, Dr. Gillespie, Dr. Greenacre, Dr. Klagsbrun, Dr. Donadello, Dr. Levy…I have only one question now: why did it have to take so long?

FELIX. You think it's them, do you?

NED. Dr. – I can't remember which one – said it would finally happen. Someone I couldn't scare away would finally show up.

FELIX. At the baths, why didn't you tell me you were a writer?

NED. Why didn't you tell me you worked for *The Times*? That I would have remembered.

FELIX. If I had told you what I did, would you have seen me again?

NED. Absolutely.

FELIX. You slut!

NED. Felix, we weren't ready then. If I had it, would you leave me?

FELIX. I don't know. Would you, if I did?

NED. No.

FELIX. How do you know?

NED. I just know. You had to have had my mother. She was a dedicated full-time social worker for the Red Cross – she put me to work on the Bloodmobile when I was eight. She was always getting an award for being best bloodcatcher or something. She's eighty now – touring China. I don't think I'm programmed any other way.

FELIX. I have something to tell you.

NED. You're pregnant.

FELIX. I was married once.

NED. Does that make me the other woman?

FELIX. I thought I was supposed to be straight. She said I had been unfair to her, which I had been. I have a son.

NED. You have a son?

FELIX. She won't let me see him.

NED. You can't see your own son? But didn't you fight? That means you're ashamed. So he will be, too.

FELIX. That's why I didn't tell you before. And who says I didn't fight! What happens to someone who cannot be as strong as you want them to be?

NED. Felix, weakness terrifies me. It scares the shit out of me. My father was weak and I'm afraid I'll be like him. His life didn't stand for anything, and then it was over. So I fight. Constantly. And if I can do it, I can't understand why everybody else can't do it, too. Okay?

FELIX. Okay.

(He pulls off one of his socks and shows NED *a purple spot on his foot.)*

It keeps getting bigger and bigger, Neddie, and it doesn't go away.

End of Act One

ACT TWO

Scene Eight

(EMMA's apartment. EMMA and NED are having brunch.)

NED. You look very pretty.

EMMA. Thank you.

NED. Where's your cat?

EMMA. Under my bed. She's afraid of you.

NED. Do you think being Jewish makes you always hungry?

EMMA. I'm not Jewish.

NED. You're not?

EMMA. I'm German.

NED. Everyone thinks you're Jewish.

EMMA. I know. In medicine that helps.

NED. How many of us do you think already have the virus in our system?

EMMA. In this city – easily over half of all gay men.

NED. So we're just walking time bombs – waiting for whatever it is that sets us off.

EMMA. Yes. And before a vaccine can be discovered almost every gay man will have been exposed. Ned, your organization is worthless! I went up and down Christopher Street last night and all I saw was guys going in the bars alone and coming out with somebody. And outside the baths, all I saw was lines of guys going in. And what is this stupid publication you finally put out? *(She holds up a pamphlet.)* After all we've talked about? You leave too much margin for intelligence. Why aren't you telling them, bluntly, stop! Every day you don't tell them, more people infect each other.

53

NED. Don't lecture me. I'm on your side. Remember?

EMMA. Don't be on my side! I don't need you on my side. Make your side shape up. I've seen 238 cases – me: one doctor. You make it sound like there's nothing worse going around than measles.

NED. They wouldn't print what I wrote. Again.

EMMA. What do you mean "they"? Who's they? thought you and Bruce were the leaders.

NED. Now we've got a board. You need a board of directors when you become tax-exempt. It was a pain in the ass finding anyone to serve on it at all! I called every prominent gay man I could get to. Forget it! Finally, what we put together turns out to be a bunch as timid as Bruce. And every time Bruce doesn't agree with me, he puts it to a board vote.

EMMA. And you lose.

NED. *(nods)* Bruce is in the closet; Mickey works for the Health Department; he starts shaking every time I criticize them – they won't even put out leaflets listing all the symptoms; Richard, Dick, and Lennie owe their jobs somehow to the Mayor; Dan is a schoolteacher; we're not allowed to say his last name out loud; the rest are just a bunch of disco dumbies. I warned you this was not a community that has its best interests at heart.

EMMA. But this is death.

NED. And the board doesn't want any sex recommendations at all. No passing along anything that isn't a hundred percent certain.

EMMA. You must tell them that's wrong! Nothing is a hundred percent certain in science, so you won't be saying anything.

NED. I think that's the general idea.

EMMA. Then why did you bother to start an organization at all?

NED. Now they've decided they only want to take care of patients – crisis counseling, support groups, home attendants...I know that's important, too. But I thought I was starting with a bunch of Ralph Naders and Green Berets, and the first instant they have to take a stand on a political issue and fight, almost in front of my eyes they turn into a bunch of nurses' aides.

EMMA. You've got to warn the living, protect the healthy, help them keep on living. I'll take care of the dying.

NED. They keep yelling at me that I can't expect an entire world to suddenly stop making love. And now I've got to tell them there's absolutely no such thing as safe sex...

EMMA. I don't consider going to the baths and promiscuous sex making love. I consider it the equivalent of eating junk food, and you can layoff it for a while. And, yes, I do expect it, and you get them to come sit in my office any day of the week and they'd expect it, too. Get a VCR, rent a porn film, and use your hands!

NED. Why are you yelling at me for what I'm not doing? What the fuck is your side doing? Where's the goddamned AMA in all of this? The government has not started one single test tube of research. Where's the board of directors of your very own hospital? You have so many patients you haven't got rooms for them, and you've got to make Felix well...So what am I yelling at you for?

EMMA. Who's Felix? Who is Felix?

NED. I introduced you to him at that Health Forum you spoke at.

EMMA. You've taken a lover?

NED. We live together. Emma, I've never been so much in love in my life. I've never been in love. Late Friday night he showed me this purple spot on the bottom of his foot. Maybe it isn't it. Maybe it's some sort of something else. It could be, couldn't it? Maybe I'm overreacting. There's so much death around. Can you see him tomorrow? I know you're booked up for weeks. But could you?

EMMA. Tell him to call me first thing tomorrow. Seven-thirty. I'll fit him in.

NED. Thank you.

EMMA. God damn you!

NED. I know I should have told you.

EMMA. What's done is done.

NED. What are we supposed to do – be with nobody ever? Well, it's not as easy as you might think. *(realizing what he's said)* Oh, Emma, I'm so sorry.

EMMA. Don't be. Polio is a virus, too. I caught it three months before the Salk vaccine was announced. Nobody gets polio anymore.

NED. Were you in an iron lung?

EMMA. For a while. But I graduated from college and from medical school first in my class. They were terrified of me. The holy terror in the wheelchair. Still are. I scare the shit out of people.

NED. I think I do, too.

EMMA. Learn how to use it. It can be very useful. Don't need everybody's love and approval.

(He embraces her impulsively; she comforts him.)

You've got to get out there on the line more than ever now.

NED. We finally have a meeting at City Hall tomorrow.

EMMA. Good. You take care of the city – I'll take care of Felix.

NED. I'm afraid to be with him; I'm afraid to be without him; I'm afraid the cure won't come in time; I'm afraid of my anger; I'm a terrible leader and a useless lover…

(He holds on to her again. Then he kisses her, breaks away from her, grabs his coat, and leaves. EMMA is alone.)

Scene Nine

*(A meeting room in City Hall. It's in a basement, windowless, dusty, a room that's hardly ever used. **NED** and **BRUCE** wait impatiently; they have been fighting. **BRUCE** wears a suit, having come from his office, with his attaché case. Both wear overcoats.)*

NED. How dare they do this to us?

BRUCE. It's one-thirty. Maybe he's not going to show up. Why don't we just leave?

NED. Keeping us down here in some basement room that hasn't been used in years. What contempt!

BRUCE. I'm sorry I let you talk me into coming here. It's not the city's responsibility to take care of us. That's why New York went broke.

NED. What we're asking for doesn't cost the city a dime: let us meet with the mayor; let him declare an emergency; have him put pressure on Washington for money for research; have him get the Times to write about us.

BRUCE. The Mayor's not going to help. Besides, if we get too political, we'll lose our tax-exempt status. That's what the lawyer in your brother's office said.

NED. You don't think the American Cancer Society, the Salvation Army, any charity you can think of, isn't somehow political, isn't putting pressure on somebody somewhere? The Catholic Church? We should be riding herd on the CDC in Atlanta – they deny it's happening in straight people, when it is. We could organize boycotts...

BRUCE. Boycotts? What in the world is there to boycott?

NED. Have you been following this Tylenol scare? In three months there have been seven deaths, and *The Times* has written fifty-four articles. The month of October alone they ran one article every single day. Four of them were on the front page. For us – in seventeen months they've written seven puny inside articles. And we have a thousand cases!

BRUCE. So?

NED. So *The Times* won't write about us, why should we read it?

BRUCE. I read it every morning. The next thing you'll say is we should stop shopping at Bloomingdale's.

NED. We should picket the White House!

BRUCE. Brilliant.

NED. Don't you have any vision of what we could become? A powerful national organization effecting change! Bruce, you must have been a fighter once. When you were a Green Beret, did you kill people?

BRUCE. A couple of times.

NED. Did you like being a soldier?

BRUCE. I loved it.

NED. Then why did you quit?

BRUCE. I didn't quit! I just don't like being earmarked gay.

NED. Bruce, what are you doing in this organization?

BRUCE. There are a lot of sick people out there that need our help.

NED. There are going to be a lot more sick people out there if we don't get our act together. Did you give up combat completely?

BRUCE. Don't you fucking talk to me about combat! I just fight different from you.

NED. I haven't seen your way yet.

BRUCE. Oh, you haven't? Where have you been?

NED. Bruce, Albert may be dying. Why doesn't that alone make you want to fight harder?

BRUCE. Get off my back!

NED. Get off your ass!

(**TOMMY** *enters.*)

TOMMY. Wonderful – we finally get a meeting with the Mayor's assistant and you two are having another fight.

BRUCE. I didn't have the fight, he had the fight. It's always Ned who has the fight.

TOMMY. Where the hell are we? What kind of tomb is this they put us in? Don't they want us to be seen above ground? Where is he? I'm an hour late.

NED. An hour and a half. And where's Mickey?

TOMMY. Not with me, lambchop. I've been up at Bellevue. I put a sweet dying child together with his momma. They hadn't seen each other for fifteen years and he'd never told her he was gay, so he didn't want to see her now. He's been refusing to see her for weeks and he was furious with me when I waltzed in with her and…It was a real weeper, Momma holding her son, and he's dead now. There are going to be a lot of mommas flying into town not understanding why their sons have suddenly upped and died from "pneumonia." You two've been barking at each other for an hour and a half? My, my.

BRUCE. Tommy, he makes me so mad.

NED. CBS called. They want our president to go on Dan Rather. He won't do it. They don't want anybody else.

BRUCE. I can't go on national television!

NED. Then you shouldn't be our president! Tommy, look at that. Imagine what a fantastic impression he would make on the whole country, speaking out for something gay. You're the kind of role model we need.

BRUCE. You want to pay me my salary and my pension and my health insurance, I'll go on TV. fired

TOMMY. Both of you, stop it. Can't you see we need both your points of view? Ned plays the bad cop and Bruce plays the good cop; every successful corporation works that way. You're both our leaders and we need you both desperately.

NED. Tommy, how is not going on national TV playing good cop?

(MICKEY enters.)

MICKEY. I couldn't get out of work. I was afraid you'd be finished by now.

BRUCE. *(to* MICKEY*)* Did you see his latest *Native* article?

MICKEY. Another one?

NED. What's so awful about what I said? It's the truth.

BRUCE. But it's how you say it!

MICKEY. What'd you say?

NED. I said we're all cowards! I said rich gays will give thousands to straight charities before they'll give us a dime. I said it is appalling that some twenty million men and women don't have one single lobbyist in Washington. How do we expect to achieve anything, ever, at all, by immaculate conception? I said the gay leaders who created this sexual-liberation philosophy in the first place have been the death of us. Mickey, why didn't you guys fight for the right to get married instead of the right to legitimize promiscuity?

MICKEY. We did!

TOMMY. I get your drift.

MICKEY. Sure you didn't leave anybody out?

NED. I said it's all our fault, everyone of us…

> (HIRAM KEEBLER, *the Mayor's assistant, enters, and* NED *carries on without a break.)*

…and you are an hour and forty-five minutes late, so why'd you bother to come at all?

BRUCE. Ned!

HIRAM. I presume I am at last having the pleasure of meeting Mr. Weeks' lilting telephone voice face to face. *(shaking hands all around)* I'm truly sorry I'm late.

MICKEY. *(shaking hands)* Michael Marcus.

HIRAM. I'm Hiram Keebler.

TOMMY. Are you related to the folks who make the crackers? Tommy Boatwright.

BRUCE. Bruce Niles.

HIRAM. The Mayor wants you to know how much he cares and how impressed he is with your superb efforts to shoulder your own responsibility.

BRUCE. Thank you.

NED. Our responsibility? Everything we're doing is stuff you should be doing. And we need help.

TOMMY. What Mr. Weeks is trying to say, sir, is that, well, we are truly swamped. We're now fielding over five hundred calls a week on our emergency hot line, people everywhere are desperate for information, which, quite frankly, the city should be providing, but isn't. We're visiting over one hundred patients each week in hospitals and homes and...

BRUCE. Sir, one thing you could help us with is office space. We're presently in one small room, and at least one hundred people come in and out every day and... no one will rent to us because of what we do and who we are.

HIRAM. That's illegal discrimination.

TOMMY. We believe we know that to be true, sir.

MICKEY. *(nervously speaking up)* Mr. Keebler, sir, it is not illegal to discriminate against homosexuals.

NED. We have been trying to see the mayor for fourteen months. It has taken us one year just to get this meeting with you and you are an hour and forty-five minutes late. Have you told the mayor there's an epidemic going on?

HIRAM. I can't tell him that!

NED. Why not?

HIRAM. Because it isn't true.

BRUCE. Yes, sir, it is.

HIRAM. Who said so?

TOMMY. The government.

HIRAM. Which government? Our government?

NED. No! Russia's government!

HIRAM. Since when?

MICKEY. The Centers for Disease Control in Atlanta declared it.

TOMMY. Seventeen months ago.

NED. How could you not know that?

HIRAM. Well, you can't expect us to concern ourselves with every little outbreak those boys come up with. And could you please reduce the level of your hysteria?

NED. Certainly. San Francisco, LA, Miami, Boston, Chicago, Washington, Denver, Houston, Seattle, Dallas – all now report cases. It's cropping up in Paris, London, Germany, Canada. But New York City, our home, the city you are pledged to protect, has over half of everything: half the one thousand cases, half the dead. Two hundred and fifty-six dead. And I know forty of them. And I don't want to know any more. And you can't not know any of this! Now – when can we see the mayor? Fourteen months is a long time to be out to lunch!

HIRAM. Now wait a minute!

NED. No, you wait a minute. We can't. Time is not on our side. If you won't take word to the Mayor, what do we do? How do we get it to him? Hire a hunky hustler and send him up to Gracie Mansion with our plea tattooed on his cock?

HIRAM. Mayor Koch is not gay!

TOMMY. Oh, come on, Blanche!

BRUCE. Tommy!

HIRAM. Now you listen to me! Of course we're aware of those figures. And before you open your big mouth again, I would like to offer you a little piece of advice. Badmouthing the Mayor is the best way I know to not get his attention.

NED. We're not getting it now, so what have we got to lose?

BRUCE. Ned!

NED. Bruce, you just heard him. Hiram here just said they're aware of the figures. And they're still not doing anything. I was worried before that they were just stupid and blind. Great! Now we get to worry about them being repressive and downright dangerous.

BRUCE. Ned! I'm sorry, sir, but we've been under a great deal of strain.

NED. (to BRUCE) Don't you ever apologize for me again. (to HIRAM) How dare you choose who will live and who will die!

HIRAM. Now listen: don't you think I want to help you? (confidentially) I have a friend who's dying from this in VA Hospital right this very minute.

NED. Then why...?

HIRAM. Because it's tricky, can't you see that? It's very tricky.

NED. Tricky, shit! There are a million gay people in New York. A million and one, counting you. That's a lot of votes. Our organization started with six men. We now have over six hundred active volunteers and a mailing list of ten thousand.

HIRAM. Six hundred? You think the mayor worries about six hundred? A fire goes out in a school furnace on the West Side between Seventy-second and Ninety-sixth streets, I get three thousand phone calls. In one day! You know what I'm talking about?

NED. Yes.

HIRAM. If so many of you are so upset about what's happening, why do I only hear from this loudmouth?

NED. That's a very good question.

HIRAM. Okay – there are half a million gay men in our area. Five hundred and nine cases doesn't seem so high, considering how many of us – I mean, of you! – there are.

NED. This is bullshit!

BRUCE. Ned! Let me take it. Sir –

HIRAM. Hiram, please. You are?

BRUCE. I'm Bruce Niles. I'm the president.

HIRAM. You're the president? What does that make Mr. Weeks here?

BRUCE. He's one of the founders.

NED. But we work together jointly.

HIRAM. Oh, you do?

NED. Yes, we do.

HIRAM. Carry on, Mr. Niles. *(He slips him his card.)*

BRUCE. Look, we realize things are tricky, but –

HIRAM. *(cutting him off)* That's right. And the Mayor feels there is no need to declare any kind of emergency. That only gets people excited. And we simply can't give you office space. We're not in the free-giveaway business.

BRUCE. We don't want it for free. We will pay for it.

HIRAM. I repeat, I think – that is, the mayor thinks you guys are overreacting.

NED. You tell that cocksucker that he's a selfish, heartless, son of a bitch!

HIRAM. You are now heading for real trouble! Do you think you can barge in here and call us names? *(to MICKEY)* You are Michael L. Marcus. You hold an unsecured job with the City Department of Health. I'd watch my step if I were you. You got yourself quite a handful here. You might consider putting him in a cage in the zoo. That I think I can arrange with the Mayor. I'd watch out for my friends here if I were you. The Mayor won't have it! *(exits)*

MICKEY. I don't believe this just happened.

NED. Mickey, I'm on the *Today Show* tomorrow and I'm going to say the Mayor is threatening your job if we don't shut up.

MICKEY. The *Today Show!* You're going to do what?!

BRUCE. You can't do that!

NED. Of course I can: he just did.

BRUCE. God damn it, Ned!

NED. We're being treated like shit. *(He yells after them as they pick up their things and leave.)* And we're allowing it. And until we force them to treat us otherwise, we get exactly what we deserve. Politicians understand only one thing-pressure! You heard him – him and his three thousand West Side phone calls. We're not yelling loud enough! Bruce, for a Green Beret, you're an awful sissy! *(He is all alone.)*

Scene Ten

(EMMA's office. FELIX sits on the examining table, wearing a white hospital gown. EMMA sits facing him.)

FELIX. So it is...it.

EMMA. Yes.

FELIX. There's not a little bit of doubt in your mind? You don't want to call in Christian Barnard?

EMMA. I'm sorry. I still don't know how to tell people. They don't teach acting in medical school.

FELIX. Aren't you worried about contagion? I mean, I assume I am about to become a leper.

EMMA. Well, I'm still here.

FELIX. Do you think they'll find a cure before I...How strange that sounds when you say it out loud for the first time.

EMMA. We're trying. But we're poor. Uncle Sam is the only place these days that can afford the kind of research that's needed, and so far we've not even had the courtesy of a reply from our numerous requests to him. You guys are still not making enough noise.

FELIX. That's Ned's department in our family. I'm not feeling too political at the moment.

EMMA. I'd like to try a treatment of several chemotherapies used together. It's milder than others. You're an early case.

FELIX. I assume that's hopeful.

EMMA. It's always better early.

FELIX. It also takes longer until you die.

EMMA. Yes. You can look at it that way.

FELIX. Do you want a second opinion?

EMMA. Feel free. But I'll say this about my fellow hospitals, you won't get particularly good care anywhere, maybe not even here. At...I'll call it Hospital A, you'll come under a group of mad scientists, research fanatics, who will try almost anything and if you die you die. You'll rarely see the same doctor twice; you'll just be a statistic for their computer – which they won't share with anyone else, by the way; there's not much sharing going on, never is. At Hospital B, they decided they really didn't want to get involved with this, it's too messy, and they're right, so you'll be overlooked by the least informed of doctors. C is like *The New York Times* and our friends everywhere: square, righteous, superior, and embarrassed by this disease and this entire epidemic. D is Catholic. E is Jewish. F is...Why am I telling you this? I must be insane. But the situation is insane.

FELIX. I guess we better get started.

EMMA. We have. You'll come to me once a week. There are going to be a lot of tests, a lot of blood tests, a lot of waiting. My secretary will give you a long list of dos and don'ts. Now, Felix, you understand your body no longer has any effective mechanism for fighting off anything?

FELIX. I'm going to be all right, you know.

EMMA. Good. That's the right attitude.

FELIX. No, I'm going to be the one who kicks it. I've always been lucky.

EMMA. Good.

FELIX. I guess everyone says that. Well, I'm going to be the one. I wanted a job on the Times, I got it. I wanted Ned...Have I given it to Ned?

EMMA. I don't know.

FELIX. Can he catch it from me now?

EMMA. We just don't know.

FELIX. Did he give it to me?

EMMA. I don't know. Only one out of a hundred adults infected with the polio virus gets it; virtually everybody infected with rabies dies. One person has a cold, hepatitis – sometimes the partner catches it, sometimes not.

FELIX. No more making love?

EMMA. Right.

FELIX. Some gay doctors are saying it's okay if you use rubbers.

EMMA. I know they are.

FELIX. Can we kiss?

EMMA. I don't know.

FELIX. *(after a long pause)* I want my mother.

EMMA. Where is she?

FELIX. She's dead. We never got along anyway.

EMMA. I'm going to do my damnedest, Felix. *(She starts to leave.)*

FELIX. Hey, Doc...I'll bet you say that to all the boys.

Scene Eleven

(A small, crowded office. Many phones are ringing.
TOMMY *is on two at once;* **MICKEY**, *going crazy, is on*
another, trying to understand and hear in the din; and
GRADY, *a volunteer, also on a phone, is trying to pass*
papers and information to either.)

MICKEY. Hello. Just a moment. It's another theory call.
Okay, go ahead. Uranus… ? *(writing it down)*

GRADY. Whose asshole you talking about, Mickey?

MICKEY. Grady!

TOMMY. *(to* **GRADY***)* I thought your friend, little Vinnie, was
going to show up today.

GRADY. He had to go to the gym.

MICKEY. *(reading into the phone what he's written)* "Mystical
electromagnetic fields ruled by the planet Uranus?"
Yes, well, we'll certainly keep that in mind. Thank you
for calling and sharing that with us.

GRADY. Harry's in a pay phone at the post office.

MICKEY. Get a number, we'll call him back.

GRADY. *(into phone)* Give me the number, I'll call you back.

TOMMY. *(into one phone)* Philip, can you hold on? *(into
second phone)* Graciella, you tell Senor Hiram I've been
holding for *diez minutos* and he called me. *Sí, sí! (into
first phone)* You know where St. Vincent's is? You get
your ass there fast! I'll send you a crisis counselor later
today. I know you're scared, honey, but just get there.

*(***GRADY*** hands ***MICKEY*** Harry's number. ***TOMMY*** has
hung up one phone.)*

MICKEY. Well, call him back!

*(***BRUCE*** comes in, dressed as from the office, with his
      _se.)*

        key, do we have a crisis counselor we can send
        around six o'clock?

        sulting a chart on a wall) No.

        . *(to* **BRUCE***)* Hi, Bossman.

BRUCE. *(answering a ringing phone)* Hello. How ya doin'! *(to the room)* It's Kessler in San Francisco.

GRADY. *(into his phone)* Louder, Harry! It's a madhouse. None of the volunteers showed up.

MICKEY. *(busying himself with paperwork)* Mystical?!

GRADY. *(on his phone)* Oh, dear.

BRUCE. *(on his)* No kidding.

GRADY. Oh, dear!

TOMMY. *(picking up a ringing phone)* Ned's not here yet.

BRUCE. *(to the room)* San Francisco's mayor is giving four million dollars to their organization. *(into phone)* Well, we still haven't met our mayor. We met with his assistant about four months ago.

TOMMY. *(to BRUCE)* Hiram called three days ago and left a message he found some money for us. Try and get him back.

MICKEY. We need to train some more crisis counselors.

GRADY. What about me, Mick?

TOMMY. *(standing up)* Okay, get this! *The Times* is finally writing a big story. Twenty months after the epidemic has been declared, *The Times* is finally writing a big story. Word is that Craig Claiborne took someone high up out to lunch and told them they really had to write something, anything.

MICKEY. Who's writing it?

TOMMY. Some lady in Baltimore.

MICKEY. Makes sense. *(His phone rings.)* Hello.

GRADY. *(still on his phone)* Oh, dear.

TOMMY. Grady, darling, what the fuck are you oh-dearing about?

GRADY. *(dropping his bombshell to BRUCE)* Bruce – Harry says the post office won't accept our mailing.

BRUCE. What! *(into phone)* Got to go. *(slams phone down and grabs GRADY's)* Harry, what's the problem?

MICKEY. *(into his phone)* That's awful.

BRUCE. *(into his phone)* They can't do that to us!

TOMMY. *(who hadn't heard* GRADY*)* What is it now?

GRADY. Harry went to the post office with the fifty-seven cartons of our new Newsletters –

TOMMY. Sugar, I sent him there!

GRADY. Well, they're not going anywhere.

BRUCE. *(to* TOMMY*)* The post office won't accept them because we just used our initials.

TOMMY. So what?

BRUCE. In order to get tax-exemption we have to use our full name.

TOMMY. There is a certain amount of irony in all this, though not right now.

GRADY. He's double-parked and his volunteers had to go home.

TOMMY. Grady, dear, would you go help him out.

GRADY. No.

TOMMY & MICKEY. Grady!

GRADY. No! Why do I always have to do the garbage stuff?

MICKEY. Grady!

GRADY. Give me the phone. *(into phone)* Hold on, Harry, I'm coming to help you. *(to* TOMMY*)* Give me cab fare.

TOMMY. Ride the rail, boy.

BRUCE. *(into the phone)* Harry, someone's coming. *(whispering to* TOMMY*)* What's his name?

TOMMY & MICKEY. Grady.

*(*GRADY *exits.)*

BRUCE. *(into phone)* Harry, bring them back. I want to fight this further somewhere. I'm sorry, I know it's a schlepp.

TOMMY. So this means we either pay full rate or embarrass their mailmen. Sorry, honey, I couldn't resist. *(into phone)* Graciella! *(to the room)* How do you say I've been holding twenty minutes in Spanish? *(into phone)* City Hall is an equal-opportunity employer, doesn't that mean you all have to learn English? *(He hangs up.)*

MICKEY. *(hanging up)* That was Atlanta. They're reporting thirty cases a week now nationally.

BRUCE. Thirty?

TOMMY. The CDC are filthy liars. What's wrong with those boys? We log forty cases a week in this office alone.

BRUCE.. Forty?

TOMMY. Forty.

MICKEY. Thirty.

BRUCE. *(trying to decide how to enter this on the wall chart)* So that's thirty nationally, forty in this office alone.

TOMMY. You heard what I said. *(dialing, then into phone)* Hi. Pick up for us, will you, dears? We need a little rest. Thank you. *(hangs up)*

> *(There is a long moment of silence, strange now without the ringing phones.* **TOMMY** *lights a cigarette and sits back.* **MICKEY** *tries to concentrate on some paperwork.* **BRUCE** *is at the wall entering figures on charts.)*

BRUCE. Mickey...aren't you supposed to be in Rio?

MICKEY. Where's Ned?

TOMMY. He should be here by now.

BRUCE. I don't want to see him.

MICKEY. I need to talk to him. I don't want to lose my job because Ned doesn't like sex very much. He's coming on like Jesus Christ, as if he never took a lover himself.

BRUCE. Rio. Why aren't you in Rio?

MICKEY. I was in Rio. I'm tired. I need a rest.

BRUCE. We're all exhausted.

TOMMY. You're the president; you can't have a rest.

MICKEY. I work all day for the city writing stuff on breast feeding versus formula and how to stay calm if you have herpes and I work all night on our Newsletter and my health columns for *The Native* and I can't take it anymore. Now this...

TOMMY. Take it slowly.

BRUCE. Now what?

MICKEY. I was in Rio, Gregory and I are in Rio, we just got there, day before yesterday, I get a phone call, from Hiram's office.

BRUCE. In Rio?

MICKEY. I'm told to be at a meeting at his office right away, this morning.

BRUCE. What kind of meeting? Why didn't you call me and I could have checked it out?

MICKEY. Because, unfortunately, you are not my boss.

BRUCE. What kind of meeting?

MICKEY. I don't know. I get to City Hall, he keeps me waiting forever; finally the Commissioner comes, my boss, and he said I hope you had a nice vacation, and went inside, into Hiram's office; and I waited some more, and the Commissioner comes out and says, Hiram doesn't want to see you anymore. I said, please, sir, then why did he make me come all the way back from Rio? He said, your vacation isn't over? I said, no sir, I was just there one day. I wanted to scream I haven't slept in two days, you dumb fuck! but I didn't. What I said was, sir, does this mean I'm fired? And the Commissioner said, no, I don't think he means that, and he left.

(NED *enters, unnoticed.*)

MICKEY. Ned's article in *The Native* attacking Hiram came out last week. I love sex! I worship men! I don't think Ned does. I don't think Ned likes himself. I –

NED. What are you trying to say, Mickey?

MICKEY. You keep trying to make us say things that we don't want to say! And I don't think we can afford to make so many enemies before we have enough friends.

NED. We'll never have enough friends. We have to accept that. And why does what I say mean I don't like myself? Why is anything I'm saying compared to anything but common sense? When are we going to have this out once and for all? How many cases a week now?

MICKEY. Thirty...forty...

NED. Reinhard dead, Craig dead, Albert sick, Felix not getting any better...Richie Faro just died.

MICKEY. Richie!

NED. That guy Ray Schwartz just committed suicide. Terry's calling all his friends from under his oxygen tent to say good-bye. Soon we're going to be blamed for not doing anything to help ourselves. When are we going to admit we might be spreading this? We have simply fucked ourselves silly for years and years, and sometimes we've done it in the filthiest places.

TOMMY. Some of us have never been to places like that, Ned.

NED. Well, good for you, Tommy. Maybe you haven't, but others you've been with have, so what's the difference?

TOMMY. *(holding up his cigarette)* It's my right to kill myself.

NED. But it is not your right to kill me. This is not a civil-rights issue, this is a contagion issue.

BRUCE. We don't know that yet, and until they discover the virus, we're not certain where this is coming from.

NED. We know enough to cool it for a while! And save lives while we do. All it takes is one wrong fuck. That's not promiscuity – that's bad luck.

TOMMY. All right, so it's back to kissing and cuddling and waiting around for Mr. Right – who could be Mr. Wrong. Maybe if they'd let us get married to begin with none of this would have happened at all. I think I'll call Dr. Ruth.

MICKEY. Will you please stop!

TOMMY. Mick, are you all right?

MICKEY. I don't think so.

TOMMY. What's wrong? Tell Tommy.

MICKEY. Why can't they find the virus?

TOMMY. It takes time.

MICKEY. I can't take any more theories. I've written a column about every single one of them. Repeated infection by a virus, new appearance by a dormant virus, single virus, new virus, old virus, multivirus, partial virus, latent virus, mutant virus, retrovirus...

TOMMY. Take it easy, honey.

MICKEY. And we mustn't forget fucking, sucking, kissing, blood, voodoo, drugs, poppers, needles, Africa, Haiti, Cuba, blacks, amebas, pigs, mosquitoes, monkeys, Uranus!...What if it isn't any of them?

TOMMY. I don't know.

MICKEY. What if it's something out of the blue? The Great Plague of London was caused by polluted drinking water from a pump nobody noticed. Maybe it's a genetic predisposition, or the theory of the herd – only so many of us will get it and then the pool's used up. What if it's monogamy? Bruce, you and I could actually be worse off because of constant bombardment of the virus from a single source – our own lovers! Maybe guys who go to the baths regularly have built up the best immunity! I don't know what to tell anybody. And everybody asks me. I don't know – who's right? I don't know – who's wrong? I feel so inadequate! How can we tell people to stop when it might turn out to be caused by – I don't know!

BRUCE. That's exactly how I feel.

MICKEY. And Ned keeps calling the Mayor a prick and Hiram a prick and the Commissioner a prick and the President and *The New York Times*, and that's the entire political structure of the entire United States! When are you going to stop your eternal name-calling at every person you see?

BRUCE. That's exactly how I feel.

MICKEY. But maybe he's right! And that scares me, too. Neddie, you scare me.

TOMMY. If I were you, I'd get back on that plane to Gregory and Rio immediately.

MICKEY. Who's going to pay my fare? And now my job. I don't make much, but it's enough to let me help out here. Where are all the gay Rockefellers? Do you think the President really wants this to happen? Do you think the CIA really has unleashed germ warfare to kill off all the queers Jerry Falwell doesn't want? Why should they help us; we're actually cooperating with them by dying?

NED. Mickey, try and hold on.

MICKEY. To what? I used to love my country. *The Native* received an anonymous letter describing top-secret Defense Department experiments at Fort Detrick, Maryland, that have produced a virus that can destroy the immune system. Its code name is Firm Hand. They started testing in 1978 – on a group of gays. I never used to believe shit like this before. They are going to persecute us! Cancel our health insurance. Test our blood to see if we're pure. Lock us up. Stone us in the streets. *(to NED)* And you think I am killing people?

NED. Mickey, that is not what I –

MICKEY. Yes, you do! I know you do! I've spent fifteen years of my life fighting for our right to be free and make love whenever, wherever...And you're telling me that all those years of what being gay stood for is wrong... and I'm a murderer. We have been so oppressed! Don't you remember how it was? Can't you see how important it is for us to love openly, without hiding and without guilt? We were a bunch of funny-looking fellows who grew up in sheer misery and one day we fell into the orgy rooms and we thought we'd found heaven. And we would teach the world how wonderful heaven can be. We would lead the way. We would be good for something new. Can't you see that? Can't you?

TOMMY. I see that. I do, Mickey. Come on – I'm taking you home now.

MICKEY. When I left Hiram's office I went to the top of the Empire State Building to jump off.

TOMMY. *(going to get* MICKEY*'s coat)* Mickey, I'm taking you home right now! Let's go.

MICKEY. You can jump off from there if no one is looking. Ned, I'm not a murderer. All my life I've been hated. For one reason or another. For being short. For being Jewish. Jerry Falwell mails out millions of pictures of two men kissing as if that was the most awful sight you could see. Tell everybody we were wrong. And I'm sorry. Someday someone will come along and put the knife in you and say everything you fought for all this time is...shit!

(He has made a furious, running lunge for NED*, but* TOMMY *catches him and cradles him in his arms.)*

BRUCE. Need any help?

TOMMY. Get my coat. *(to* MICKEY*)* You're just a little tired, that's all, a little bit yelled out. We've got a lot of different styles that don't quite mesh. We've got ourselves a lot of bereavement overload. Tommy's taking you home.

MICKEY. No, don't take me home. I'm afraid I might do something. Take me to St. Vincent's. I'm just afraid.

TOMMY. I'll take you wherever you want to go. *(to* BRUCE *and* NED*)* Okay, you two, no more apologizing and no more fucking excuses. You two better start accommodating and talking to each other now. Or we're in big trouble.

MICKEY. We're the fighters, aren't we?

TOMMY. You bet, sweetness. And you're a hero. Whether you know it or not. You're our first hero.

*(*TOMMY *and* MICKEY *leave. There is a long moment of silence.)*

NED. We're all going to go crazy, living this epidemic every minute, while the rest of the world goes on out there, all around us, as if nothing is happening, going on with their own lives and not knowing what it's like, what we're going through. We're living through war, but where they're living it's peacetime, and we're all in the same country.

BRUCE. Do you want to be president?

NED. I just want Felix to live. *(A phone on* **TOMMY***'s desk rings.)* Hello. Hiram, old buddy, how they hanging? I want to talk to you, too. *(He listens, then hangs up softly.)* Tommy's right. All yelled out. You ready?

BRUCE. Yes.

NED. The Mayor has found a secret little fund for giving away money. But we're not allowed to tell anyone where we got it. If word gets out we've told, we won't get it.

BRUCE. How much?

NED. Nine thousand dollars.

BRUCE. Ned, Albert is dead.

NED. Oh, no.

BRUCE. What's today?

NED. Wednesday.

BRUCE. He's been dead a week.

NED. I didn't know he was so close.

BRUCE. No one did. He wouldn't tell anyone. Do you know why? Because of me. Because he knows I'm so scared I'm some sort of carrier. This makes three people I've been with who are dead. I went to Emma and I begged her: please test me somehow, please tell me if I'm giving this to people. And she said she couldn't, there isn't any way they can find out anything because they still don't know what they're looking for. Albert, I think I loved him best of all, and he went so fast. His mother wanted him back in Phoenix before he died, this was last week when it was obvious, so I get permission from Emma and bundle him all up and take him to the plane in an ambulance. The pilot wouldn't take off and I refused to leave the plane – you would have been proud of me – so finally they get another pilot. Then, after we take off, Albert loses his mind, not recognizing me, not knowing where he is or that he's going home, and then, right there, on the plane, he becomes…incontinent. He starts doing it in his pants

and all over the seat; shit, piss, everything. I pulled
down my suitcase and yanked out whatever clothes
were in there and I start mopping him up as best I
can, and all these people are staring at us and moving
away in droves and…I ram all these clothes back in
the suitcase and I sit there holding his hand, saying,
"Albert, please, no more, hold it in, man, I beg you,
just for us, for Bruce and Albert." And when we got
to Phoenix, there's a police van waiting for us and all
the police are in complete protective rubber clothing,
they looked like fucking astronauts, and by the time
we got to the hospital where his mother had fixed up
his room real nice, Albert was dead. (**NED** *starts toward
him.*) Wait. It gets worse. The hospital doctors refused
to examine him to put a cause of death on the death
certificate, and without a death certificate the under-
takers wouldn't take him away, and neither would
the police. Finally, some orderly comes in and stuffs
Albert in a heavy-duty Glad Bag and motions us with
his finger to follow and he puts him out in the back
alley with the garbage. He says, "Hey, man. See what a
big favor I've done for you, I got him out, I want fifty
bucks." I paid him and then his mother and I carried
the bag to her car and we finally found an undertaker
who cremated him for a thousand dollars, no questions asked.

(**NED** *crosses to* **BRUCE** *and embraces him;* **BRUCE** *puts
his arms around* **NED**.)

Would you and Felix mind if I spent the night on your
sofa? Just one night. I don't want to go home.

Scene Twelve

(**EMMA** *sits alone in a spotlight, facing a doctor who stands at a distance, perhaps in the audience. She holds a number of files on her lap, or they are placed in a carrier attached to her wheelchair.*)

EXAMINING DOCTOR. Dr. Brookner, the government's position is this. There are several million dollars in the pipeline, five to be exact, for which we have received some fifty-five million dollars' worth of requests – all the way from a doctor in North Dakota who desires to study the semen of pigs to the health reporter on Long Island who is convinced this is being transmitted by dogs and the reason so many gay men are contracting it is because they have so many dogs.

EMMA. Five million dollars doesn't seem quite right for some two thousand cases. The government spent twenty million investigating seven deaths from Tylenol. We are now almost into the third year of this epidemic.

EXAMINING DOCTOR. Unfortunately President Reagan has threatened to veto. As you know, he's gone on record as being unalterably and irrevocably opposed to anything that might be construed as an endorsement of homosexuality. Naturally, this has slowed things down.

EMMA. Naturally. It looks like we've got a pretty successful stalemate going on here.

EXAMINING DOCTOR. Well, that's not what we're here to discuss today, is it?

EMMA. I don't think I'm going to enjoy hearing what I think I'm about to hear. But go ahead. At your own peril.

EXAMINING DOCTOR. We have decided to reject your application for funding.

EMMA. Oh? I would like to hear your reasons.

EXAMINING DOCTOR. We felt the direction of your thinking was imprecise and unfocused.

EMMA. Could you be a little more precise?

EXAMINING DOCTOR. I beg your pardon?

EMMA. You don't know what's going on any more than
I do. My guess is as good as anybody's. Why are you
blocking my efforts?

EXAMINING DOCTOR. Dr. Brookner, since you first became
involved with this – and we pay tribute to you as a pio-
neer, one of the few courageous pioneers – there have
been other investigators...Quite frankly, it's no longer
just your disease, though you seem to think it is.

EMMA. Oh, I do, do I? And you're here to take it away
from me, is that it? Well, I'll let you in on a little
secret, doctor. You can have it. I didn't want it in the
first place. You think it's my good fortune to have the
privilege of watching young men die? Oh, what's the
use! What am I arguing with you for? You don't know
enough medicine to treat a mouse. You don't know
enough science to study boiled water. How dare you
come and judge me?

EXAMINING DOCTOR. We only serve on this panel at the
behest of Dr. Joost.

EMMA. Another idiot. And, by the way, a closeted homo-
sexual who is doing everything in his power to sweep
this under the rug, and I vowed I'd never say that in
public. How does it always happen that all the idiots
are always on your team? You guys have all the money,
call the shots, shut everybody out, and then operate
behind closed doors. I am taking care of more vic-
tims of this epidemic than anyone in the world. We
have more accumulated test results, more data, more
frozen blood samples, more experience! How can you
not fund my research or invite me to participate in
yours? A promising virus has already been discovered
– in France. Why are we being told not to cooperate
with the French? Why are you refusing to cooperate
with the French? Just so you can steal a Nobel Prize?
Your National Institutes of Health received my first
request for research money two years ago. It took
you one year just to print up application forms. It's

taken you two and a half years from my first reported case just to show up here to take a look. The paltry amount of money you are making us beg for – from the four billion dollars you are given each and every year – won't come to anyone until only God knows when. Any way you add all this up, it is an unconscionable delay and has never, never existed in any other health emergency during this entire century. While something is being passed around that causes death. We are enduring an epidemic of death. Women have been discovered to have it in Africa – where it is clearly transmitted heterosexually. It is only a question of time. We could all be dead before you do anything. You want my patients? Take them! TAKE THEM! *(She starts hurling her folders and papers at him, out into space.)* Just do something for them! You're fucking right I'm imprecise and unfocused. And you are all idiots!

Scene Thirteen

(A big empty room, which will be the organization's new offices. BRUCE is walking around by himself. NED comes in from upstairs.)

NED. This is perfect for our new offices. The room upstairs is just as big. And it's cheap.

BRUCE. How come, do you think?

NED. Didn't Tommy tell you? After he found it, he ran into the owner in a gay bar who confessed, after a few beers, his best friend is sick. Did you see us on TV picketing the Mayor yesterday in all that rain?

BRUCE. Yes.

NED. How'd we look?

BRUCE. All wet.

NED. He's got four more hours to go. Our letter threatened if he didn't meet with us by the end of the day we'd escalate the civil disobedience. Mel found this huge straight black guy who trained with Martin Luther King. He's teaching us how to tie up the bridge and tunnel traffic. Don't worry – a bunch of us are doing this on our own.

BRUCE. Tommy got the call.

NED. Tommy? Why didn't you tell me? When did they call?

BRUCE. This morning.

NED. When's the meeting?

BRUCE. Tomorrow.

NED. You see. It works! What time?

BRUCE. Eight A.M.

NED. For the Mayor I'll get up early.

BRUCE. We can only bring ten people. Hiram's orders.

NED. Who's going?

BRUCE. The Community Council sends two, the Network sends two, the Task Force sends two, we send two, and two patients.

NED. I'll pick you up at seven-thirty and we can share a cab.

BRUCE. You remember we elected Tommy executive director.

NED. I'm going.

BRUCE. We can only bring two.

NED. You just call Hiram and tell him we're bringing three.

BRUCE. The list of names has already been phoned in. It's too late.

NED. So I'll just go. What are they going to do? Kick me out? Already phoned in? Too late? Why is everything so final? Why is all this being done behind my back? How dare you make this decision without consulting me?

BRUCE. Ned...

NED. I wrote that letter, I got sixty gay organizations to sign it, I organized the picketing when the Mayor wouldn't respond, that meeting is mine! It's happening because of me! It took me twenty-one months to arrange it and, God damn it, I'm going to go!

BRUCE. You're not the whole organization.

NED. What does that mean? Why didn't Tommy tell me?

BRUCE. I told him not to.

NED. You what?

BRUCE. I wanted to poll the board.

NED. Behind my back – what kind of betrayal is going on behind my back? I'm on the board, you didn't poll me. I am going to that meeting representing this organization that I have spent every minute of my life fighting for and that was started in my living room, or I quit!

BRUCE. I told them I didn't think you'd accept their decision.

NED. *(as it sinks in)* You would let me quit? You didn't have to poll the board. If you wanted to take me, you'd take me. I embarrass you.

BRUCE. Yes, you do. The Mayor's finally meeting with us and we all feel we now have a chance to –

NED. A chance to kiss his ass?

BRUCE. We want to work from the inside now that we have the contact.

NED. It won't work. Did you get this meeting by kissing his ass? He's the one person most responsible for letting this epidemic get so out of control. If he'd responded with one ounce of compassion when we first tried to reach him, we'd have saved two years. You'll see... We have over half a million dollars. *The Times* is finally writing about us. Why are you willing to let me go when I've been so effective? When you need me most?

BRUCE. You...you're a bully. If the board doesn't agree with you, you always threaten to leave. You never listen to us. I can't work with you anymore.

NED. And you're strangling this organization with your fear and your conservatism. The organization I promised everyone would fight for them isn't fighting at all.

BRUCE. Maybe it's become what it wanted to become. Maybe that's all it could become. You can't turn something into something it doesn't want to become. We just feel you can't tell people how to live.

NED. Drop that! Just drop it! The cases are still doubling every six months. Of course we have to tell people how to live. Or else there won't be any people left! Did you ever consider it could get so bad they'll quarantine us or put us in camps?

BRUCE. Oh, they will not.

NED. It's happened before. It's all happened before. History is worth shit. I swear to God I now understand... Is this how so many people just walked into gas chambers? But at least they identified themselves to each other and to the world.

BRUCE. You can't call people gay who don't want to be.

NED. Bruce – after you're dead, it doesn't make any difference.

BRUCE. *(takes a letter out of his pocket)* The board wanted me to read you this letter. "We are circulating this letter widely among people of judgment and good sense in our community. We take this action to try to combat your damage, wrought, so far as we can see, by your having no scruples whatever. You are on a colossal ego trip we must curtail. To manipulate fear, as you have done repeatedly in your 'merchandising' of this epidemic, is to us the gesture of barbarism. To exploit the deaths of gay men, as you have done in publications all over America, is to us an act of inexcusable vandalism. And to attempt to justify your bursts of outrageous temper as 'part of what it means to be Jewish' is past our comprehending. And, after years of liberation, you have helped make sex dirty again for us – terrible and forbidden. We are more angry at you than ever in our lives toward anyone. We think you want to lead us all. Well, we do not want you to. In accordance with our by-laws as drawn up by Weeks, Frankel, Levinstein, Mr. Ned Weeks is hereby removed as a director. We beg that you leave us quietly and not destroy us and what good work we manage despite your disapproval. In closing, please know we always welcome your input, advice, and help."

(BRUCE tries to hand NED the letter. NED won't take it. BRUCE tries to put it in NED's breast pocket. NED deflects BRUCE's hand.)

NED. I belong to a culture that includes Proust, Henry James, Tchaikovsky, Cole Porter, Plato, Socrates, Aristotle, Alexander the Great, Michelangelo, Leonardo da Vinci, Christopher Marlowe, Walt Whitman, Herman Melville, Tennessee Williams, Byron, E.M. Forster, Lorca, Auden, Francis Bacon, James Baldwin, Harry Stack Sullivan, John Maynard Keynes, Dag Hammarskjold…These are not invisible men. Poor Bruce. Poor frightened Bruce. Once upon a time you wanted to be a soldier. Bruce, did you know that an openly gay Englishman was as responsible as any man for winning the Second World War? His name was Alan Turing and he cracked the Germans' Enigma code so the Allies knew in advance what the Nazis were going to do – and when the war was over he committed suicide he was so hounded for being gay. Why don't they teach any of this in the schools? If they did, maybe he wouldn't have killed himself and maybe you wouldn't be so terrified of who you are. The only way we'll have real pride is when we demand recognition of a culture that isn't just sexual. It's all there – all through history we've been there; but we have to claim it, and identify who was in it, and articulate what's in our minds and hearts and all our creative contributions to this earth. And until we do that, and until we organize ourselves block by neighborhood by city by state into a united visible community that fights back, we're doomed. That's how I want to be defined: as one of the men who fought the war. Being defined by our cocks is literally killing us. Must we all be reduced to becoming our own murderers? Why couldn't you and I, Bruce Niles and Ned Weeks, have been leaders in creating a new definition of what it means to be gay? I blame myself as much as you. Bruce, I know I'm an asshole. But, please, I beg you, don't shut me out.

(**BRUCE** *starts to leave then stops and comes to* **NED**. *He puts his hand on his cheek, perhaps kisses him, and then leaves him standing alone.*)

Scene Fourteen

(NED's apartment. FELIX is sitting on the floor. He has been eating junk food. NED comes in carrying a bag of groceries.)

NED. Why are you sitting on the floor?

FELIX. I fell down trying to get from there to here.

NED. Let's put you to bed.

FELIX. Don't touch me! I'm so ugly. I cannot stand it when you look at my body.

NED. Did you go to chemo today?

FELIX. Yes. I threw it all up. You don't have to let me stay here with you. This is horrible for you.

NED. *(touching FELIX's hair)* No fallout yet. Phil looks cute shaved. I'm hungry. How about you? Can you eat a little? Please. You've got to eat. Soup...something light...I've bought dinner.

FELIX. Emma says a cure won't come until the next century. Emma says it's years till a vaccine, which won't do me any good anyway. Emma says the incubation period might be up to three, ten, twenty years.

NED. Emma says you've got to eat.

FELIX. I looked at all my datebooks and no one else I slept with is sick. That I know of. Maybe it was you. Maybe you've been a carrier for twenty years. Or maybe now you only have three years to go.

NED. Felix, we don't need to do this again to each other.

FELIX. Whoever thought you'd die from having sex?

NED. Did Emma also tell you that research at the NIH has finally started. That something is now possible. We have to hope.

FELIX. Oh, do we?

NED. Yes, we do.

FELIX. And how am I supposed to do that? You Jewish boys who think you can always make everything right – that the world can always be a better place. Did I tell you *The Times* is running an editorial this Sunday entitled "The Slow Response"? And you're right: I didn't have anything to do with it.

NED. Why are you doing this? Why are you eating this shit? Twinkies, potato chips... You know how important it is to watch your nutrition. You're supposed to eat right.

FELIX. I have a life expectancy of ten more minutes I'm going to eat what I want to eat. Ned, it's going to get messier any day now and I don't want to make you see it.

NED. Nobody makes me do anything; you should know that better than anybody else by now. What are you going to do? Sit on the floor for the rest of your life? We have a bed in the other room. You could listen to those relaxation tapes we bought you three months ago. You haven't used them at all. Do you hear me?

NED. Yes, I hear you. That guy David who sold you the pig on Bleecker Street finally died. He took forever. They say he looked like someone out of Auschwitz. Do you hear me?

NED. No. Are you ready to get up yet? And eat something?

FELIX. No! – I've had over forty treatments. No! I've had three, no four different types of chemo. No! – I've had interferon, a couple kinds. I've had two different experimentals. Emma has spent more time on me than anyone else. None of it has done a thing. I've had to go into the hospital four times – and please God don't make me go back into the hospital until I die. My illness has cost my – no! *The New York Times*' insurance company over $300,000. Eighty-five percent of us are dead after two years, Alexander; it gets higher after three. Emma has lost so many patients they call her Dr. Death. You cannot force the goddamn sun to come out.

NED. Felix, I am so sick of statistics, and numbers, and body counts, and how-manys, and Emma; and everyday, Felix, there are only more numbers, and fights – I am so sick of fighting, and bragging about fighting, and everybody's stupidity, and blindness, and intransigence, and guilt trips. You can't eat the food? Don't eat the food. Take your poison. I don't care. You can't get up off the floor – fine, stay there. I don't care. Fish – fish is good for you; we don't want any of that, do we? *(Item by item, he throws the food on the floor.)* No green salad. No broccoli; we don't want any of that, no, sir. No bread with seven grains. Who would ever want any milk? You might get some calcium in your bones. *(The carton of milk explodes when it hits the floor.)* You want to die, Felix? Die!

*(*NED *retreats to a far corner. After a moment,* FELIX *crawls through the milk, and with extreme effort makes his way across to* NED. *They fall into each other's arms.)*

Felix, please don't leave me.

Scene Fifteen

(BEN's office. FELIX, with great effort, walks toward him. Though he looks terrible, FELIX has a bit of his old twinkle.)

FELIX. Thank you for seeing me. Your brother and I are lovers. I'm dying and I need to make a will. Oh, I know Neddie hasn't been talking to you; our excuse is we've sort of been preoccupied. It's a little hard on us, isn't it, his kind of love, because we disappoint him so. But it is love. I hope you know that. I haven't very much time left. I want to leave everything to Ned. I've written it all down.

BEN. *(taking the piece of paper from FELIX and studying it)* Do you have any family, Felix?

FELIX. My parents are dead. I had a wife.

BEN. You had a wife?

FELIX. Yes. Here's the divorce. *(He hands BEN another piece of paper.)* And I have a son. Here's...she has custody. *(He hands over yet another piece of paper.)*

BEN. Does she know you're ill?

FELIX. Yes. I called and we've said our good-byes. She says she doesn't want anything from me. She was actually rather pleasant. Although she wouldn't let me talk to my boy.

BEN. How is my brother?

FELIX. Well, he blames himself, of course, for everything from my dying to the state of the entire world. But he's not talking so much these days, believe it or not. You must be as stubborn as he is – not to have called.

BEN. I think of doing it every day. I'm sorry I didn't know you were ill. I'll call him right away.

FELIX. He's up at Yale for the week. He's in terrible shape. He was thrown out of the organization he loved so much. After almost three years he sits at home all day, flagellating himself awfully because he thinks he's failed some essential test – plus my getting near the end and you two still not talking to each other.

BEN. Ned was thrown out of his own organization?

FELIX. Yes.

BEN. Felix, I wish we could have met sooner.

FELIX. I haven't much, except a beautiful piece of land on the Cape in Wellfleet on a hill overlooking the Atlantic Ocean. Ned doesn't know about it. It was to have been a surprise, we'd live there together in the house he always wanted. I also have an insurance policy with *The Times*. I'm a reporter for *The New York Times*.

BEN. You work for *The Times*?

FELIX. Yes. Fashion. La-de-da. It's meant to come to my next of kin. I've specified Ned. I'm afraid they might not give it to him.

BEN. If he is listed as the beneficiary, they must.

FELIX. But what if they don't?

BEN. I assure you I will fight to see that he gets it.

FELIX. I was hoping you'd say that. Can I sign my will now, please, in case I don't have time to see you again?

BEN. This will be quite legal. We can stop by one of my associates' offices and get it properly witnessed as you sign it.

FELIX. My little piece of paper is legal? Then why did you go to law school?

BEN. I sometimes wonder. You know, Felix, I think of leaving here, too, because I don't think anybody is listening to me either. And I set all this up as well. I understand that the virus has finally been discovered in Washington.

FELIX. The story is they couldn't find it, so after fifteen months they stole it from the French and renamed it. With who knows how many millions of us now exposed…Oh, there is not a good word to be said for anybody's behavior in this whole mess. Then could you help me get a taxi, please? I have to get to the airport.

BEN. The airport?

FELIX. I'm going to Rumania to see their famous woman doctor. A desperation tactic, Tommy would call it. Does flying Bucharest Airlines inspire you with any confidence?

Scene Sixteen

(**FELIX**'s *hospital room.* **FELIX** *lies in bed.* **NED** *enters.*)

FELIX. I should be wearing something white.

NED. You are.

FELIX. It should be something Perry Ellis ran up for me personally.

NED. *(as* **FELIX** *presses a piece of rock into his hand)* What's this?

FELIX. From my trip. I forgot to give it to you. This is a piece of rock from Dracula's castle.

NED. Reminded you of me, did it?

FELIX. To remind you of me. Please learn to fight again.

NED. I went to a meeting at the Bishop's. All the gay leaders were there, including Bruce and Tommy. I wasn't allowed in. I went in to the men's room of the rectory and the Bishop came in and as we stood there peeing side by side I screamed at him, "What kind of house of God are we in?"

FELIX. Don't lose that anger. Just have a little more patience and forgiveness. For yourself as well.

NED. What am I ever going to do without you?

FELIX. Finish writing something. Okay?

NED. Okay.

FELIX. Promise?

NED. I promise.

FELIX. Okay. It better be good.

(**BEN** *enters the scene.*)

Hello, Ben.

BEN. Hello, Felix.

(*Before* **NED** *can do more than register his surprise at seeing* **BEN**, **EMMA** *enters and comes to the side of the bed.*)

FELIX. Emma, could we start, please.

EMMA. We are gathered here in the sight of God to join together these two men. They love each other very much and want to be married in the presence of their family before Felix dies. I can see no objection. This is my hospital, my church. Do you, Felix Turner, take Ned Weeks –

FELIX. Alexander.

EMMA. ...to be your...

FELIX. My lover. My lover. I do.

NED. I do.

(FELIX *is dead.* EMMA, *who has been holding* FELIX*'s hand and monitoring his pulse, places his hand on his body. She leaves.* TWO ORDERLIES *enter and push the hospital bed, through all the accumulated mess, off stage.*)

He always wanted me to take him to your new house in the country. Just the four of us.

BEN. Ned, I'm sorry. For Felix...and for other things.

NED. Why didn't I fight harder! Why didn't I picket the White House, all by myself if nobody would come. Or go on a hunger strike. I forgot to tell him something. Felix, when they invited me to Gay Week at Yale, they had a dance...In my old college dining hall, just across the campus from that tiny freshman room where I tried to kill myself because I thought I was the only gay man in the world – they had a dance. Felix, there were six hundred young men and women there. Smart, exceptional young men and women.

(*pause*)

Thank you, Felix.

(*After a moment,* BEN *crosses to* NED, *and somehow they manage to kiss and embrace and hold on to each other.*)

The End

AFTERWORD

*A copy of this letter was given to every member of
the audience as they left the theatre.*

A Letter from Larry Kramer

PLEASE KNOW

Thank you for coming to see our play.

Please know that everything in *The Normal Heart* happened. These were and are real people who lived and spoke and died, and are presented here as best I could. Several more have died since, including Bruce, whose name was Paul Popham, and Tommy, whose name was Rodger McFarlane and who became my best friend, and Emma, whose name was Dr. Linda Laubenstein of New York University Medical Center. She died after a return bout of polio and another trip to an iron lung. Rodger, after building three gay/AIDS agencies from the ground up, committed suicide in despair. On his deathbed at Memorial, Paul called me (we'd not spoken since our last fight in this play) and told me to never stop fighting.

Four members of the original cast died as well, including my dear sweet friend Brad Davis, the original Ned, whom I knew from practically the moment he got off the bus from Florida, a shy kid intent on becoming a fine actor, which he did.

Please know that AIDS is a worldwide plague.

Please know that no country in the world, including this one, especially this one, has ever called it a plague, or dealt with it as a plague.

Please know that there is no cure.

Please know that after all this time the amount of money being spent to find a cure is still miniscule, still almost invisible, still impossible to locate in any national health budget, and still totally uncoordinated.

Please know that here in America case numbers continue to rise in every category. In much of the rest of the world, like Russia, India, Southeast Asia, and in Africa, the numbers of the infected and the dying are so grotesquely high they are rarely acknowledged.

Please know that all efforts at prevention and educations continue their unending record of abject failure.

Please know that there is no one in charge of this plague. This is a war for which there is no general and for which there has never been a general. How can you win a war with no one in charge?

Please know that beginning with Ronald Reagan (who would not say the word AIDS publicly for seven years), every single president has said nothing and done nothing, or in the case of the current president, says the right things and then doesn't do them.

Please know that most medications for HIV/AIDS are inhumanly expensive and that government funding for the poor to obtain them is twindling and often unavailable.

Please know that pharmaceutical companies are among the most evil and greedy nightmares ever loosed on humankind. What research they embark upon is calculated only toward finding newer drugs to keep us, just barely, from dying, but not to make us better or, god forbid, cured.

Please know that an awful lot of people have needlessly died and will continue to needlessly die because of any and all of the above.

Please know that as I write this the world has suffered at the very least some 75 million infections and 35 million deaths. When the action of the play that you have just seen begins, there were 41.

I have never seen such wrongs as this plague, in all its guises, represents, and continues to say about us all.

Larry Kramer,
July 2011

ABOUT THE PLAYWRIGHT

In 1981, with five friends, Larry Kramer founded Gay Men's Health Crisis, still one of the world's largest provider of services to those with AIDS. In 1987, he founded ACT UP, the AIDS advocacy and protest organization, which has been responsible for the development and release of almost every life-saving treatment for HIV/AIDS.

He is the author of *The Normal Heart*, which was selected as one of the 100 Greatest Plays of the Twentieth Century by the Royal National Theatre of Great Britain and is the longest running play in the history of the New York Shakespeare Festival's Public Theater. He is also the author of *The Destiny of Me*, which was a finalist for the Pulitzer Prize and won an Obie and the Lucille Lortel Award for Best Play. Kramer's screenplay adaptation of D.H. Lawrence's *Women in Love*, a film he also produced, was nominated for an Academy Award. His writing about AIDS is published in *Reports from the holocaust: the story of an AIDS activist*, and *The Tragedy of Today's Gays*. His novel, *Faggots*, is one of the bestselling of all gay novels. He is a recipient of the Award in Literature from the American Academy of Arts and Letters and he was the first openly gay person and the first creative artist to be honored by an award from Common Cause.

The American People, which Kramer has been working on since 1975 and is now some 4000 pages long, will be published by Farrar Straus and Giroux.

A graduate of Yale, Kramer lives in New York and Connecticut with his lover, architect/designer David Webster.

See what people are saying about
THE NORMAL HEART...

"The staging is both stripped-down and dramatically full-bodied;
it has a scorching eloquence that admirably serves the rage and
anguish of Larry Kramer's text."
– *The Hollywood Reporter*

"A spectacular and spectacularly moving revival."
– *The New York Observer*

"If you see only one play this year, make it *The Normal Heart!*"
– *Backstage*

"Run to *The Normal Heart* if you want to be reminded of how alive
you are!"
– *The Village Voice*

"Hits you like a jackhammer. A powerful example of theater at its
most direct, passionate and urgent. Devastating."
– *AM New York*

"Riveting theater!"
– *Newsday*

"A stunning Broadway revival. This is essentially Ibsen for our
times. The play's complexity is brought to pulse-pounding life! The
entire company acts up a storm, and the production leaves you
drenched. Raw, scary and galvanizing."
– *Time Out New York*

"Scalding and poignant. It is a breathtaking achievement. Period."
– *Daily News*

"*The Normal Heart* is breathing fire again! A great cathartic night at
the theater!"
– *The New York Times*

Also by
Larry Kramer...

Just Say No

The Destiny of Me

Please visit our website **samuelfrench.com** for complete
descriptions and licensing information.

OTHER TITLES AVAILABLE FROM SAMUEL FRENCH

JUST SAY NO

Larry Kramer

Comedy / 5m, 3f / Interior

The scandals of the Reagan administration are dramatized in farcical style. The First Lady must locate, before it is too late, a home made sex videotape on which she cavorts with the husband of her best friend, with his mistress who knows much too much, and with members of her husband's cabinet. In addition, her son decides to run away to become a ballet dancer and, along the way, falls in love with the ex boyfriend in hiding of the angry mayor of the largest northeastern city. Everyone meets, or tries not to, in the Georgetown home of Foppy Schwartz, friend to the rich and powerful, where first ladies and mayors drop in and refuse to leave. *Just Say No* is a hysterically funny satire that has a great deal to say about the state of our union.

"Beneath the brittle, pun filled dialogue, Kramer's rage against people in high places simmers. The dialogue is deliriously artificial and crackling."
– *The New York Times*

"*Just Say No* risks everything by turning rage to farce and back again. I'm ready to go anywhere Kramer wishes to take me."
– *Village Voice*

OTHER TITLES AVAILABLE FROM SAMUEL FRENCH

THE DESTINY OF ME

Larry Kramer

Drama / 5m, 2f / Unit Set

Gay activist Larry Kramer scored a triumph in New York with this absorbing sequel to *The Normal Heart*. Ned Weeks, having lost his lover to AIDS, has tested HIV positive and has checked into a hospital to begin treatment. He battles with the medical establishment even as he battles his past in this memory play in the tradition of *The Glass Menagerie*. Moving fluidly from present to past and back again, *The Destiny of Me* reveals the young Alexander who grows up to be Ned, his coming to terms with his homosexuality and his family's reluctance to do so.

"Full of moments that tear at the heart."
– *Variety*

"Bitter and angry and full of the biting humor that comes not from a joy of life but from trying to make the best of it."
– *Wall Street Journal*

"May be the most comprehending, and certainly the most comprehensive, AIDS play so far."
– *New York Magazine*

"This play will stand as a memorial to the personal force of a single man and to a fearful trauma in American life."
– *Newsweek*

SAMUELFRENCH.COM

OTHER TITLES AVAILABLE FROM SAMUEL FRENCH

BOYS IN THE BAND

Mart Crowley

Drama / 9m / Interior

This seminal work of the Off-Broadway movement premiered in 1968 and was a long-running hit onstage, later filmed with the original cast. In 2010, the play made a triumphant return to New York City in an highly praised production produced by Drama Desk and Obie Award winning Transport Group.

In his upper eastside Manhattan apartment, Michael is throwing a birthday party for Harold, a self-awoved "32 year-old, pock-marked, Jew fairy", complete with surprise gift: "Cowboy" a street hustler. As the evening wears on, fueled by drugs and alcohol, bitter, unresolved resentments among the guests come to light when a game of "Truth" goes terribly wrong.

"A play of real substance, one that deserves to be performed not occasionally but regularly."
–The Wall Street Journal

"...terrifically thoughtful...*The Boys in the Band* emerges remarkably universal."
– NY1

"...deliriously delicious..."
– Gay City News

"*The Boys in the Band* goes from wittily bitchy to heartbreakingly brutal..."
– Out Magazine

"Witty, bitchy, revelatory and dazzlingly entertaining...the excoriating wit is still there."
– New York Post

SAMUELFRENCH.COM

CPSIA information can be obtained
at www.ICGtesting.com
Printed in the USA
BVOW09s1417200418
513853BV00001B/20/P